Editing: Twisting Curses
Cover art: Ryuu Kosayase

This is a work of fiction. Names, characters, businesses, places, events, locales, and incidents are either the products of the author's imagination or used in a fictitious manner. Any resemblance to actual persons, living or dead, or actual events is purely coincidental.

Copyright © 2022 Michael D. Cinder

All rights reserved. No part of this book may be reproduced or used in any manner without the prior written permission of the copyright owner, except for the use of brief quotations in a book review.

If you enjoy this novel, please leave a review and/or drop me a line at:
Michael.D.Cinder@gmail.com

Table of Contents

CHAPTER 1

Valentina - STS Arcadia in route to Europa

Time and luck were running out for Valentina Victorovna. At any moment, the security team aboard the *STS Arcadia* could find her. The storage closet full of pressure suits she'd chosen to hide away in now seemed like a dead end. Her eyes were locked on the door as her imagination ran wild. She had been so careful not to catch the attention of the *Arcadia*'s crew. She was a stowaway on the vessel's month-long journey to Europa. She had no idea what they did with "free passengers." The morbid thought of being shot out of an airlock was better than the alternative she kept revisiting in her mind.

Valentina's anxiety was running rampant, causing her to lose mental focus and her muscles to tense to the point of aching. Her mind focused on how she spent too much time in the mess hall today. She cursed herself for asking for one extra ration. That single question borne out of hunger invited the cook to ask her name and what room she was quartered in so he could send along additional food if she needed it. She'd lied to the former, providing the name of "Susan", while waving off the cook's intentions. He had shrugged the whole notion off with a practiced smile, yet Valentina couldn't stop envisioning him talking with ship security about the incident. Now they were looking for her.

The small portion of her mind that was still rational knew she was jumping at shadows. Though with good reason. After all, the heiress to the Kukleva Cosmonautical faction had endured countless betrayals, assassination attempts, false friends, and more during her life. The difference was she knew how to see those sorts of things coming and avoid them entirely. Here, in a foreign environment with no lifelines to call upon, she was out of her element. But that was the point. How else was she supposed to ensure that her arranged-spouse couldn't find her on her way out into the sticks of the solar system?

The thought of her arranged-spouse and all the terror that came with it left Valentina a shaking mess. After a few tense hours she finally allowed herself to breathe and relax. There was no way Rolf Wesler could know she was aboard. She had pulled every reliable connection and favor to mask her stowing away on the *Arcadia*. No paper trails and only the absolute essentials in terms of carry-ons. She had to be safe, right?

A burst of static from a loudspeaker outside her hiding spot caused her to nearly leap out of her skin. She missed the beginning of what the captain of the *Arcadia* was saying as she forced herself to calm down and listen:

"...approximately an hour until we will be docking with Europa's Light Lift. Local time is 6500 hours. Surface temperature is a balmy -163° C. Please ensure you take everything with you when you disembark. Those leaving behind a mess or forgetting items will be charged an additional fee as stipulated in the contract you signed back on Earth. On behalf of the crew of the *Arcadia*, we hope your journey has been a pleasant one..."

Valentina let out her held breath, only to regret it moments later. A new voice, one of an actual person outside the storage closet, stole the remaining air from her lungs.

"I wonder where the leak is," said a bored-sounding, gruff man. "It's definitely on this deck but this stupid thing isn't working."

The sound of flesh smacking a piece of equipment was followed by a feminine laugh from a second individual, "That's because you keep hitting it! Here, let me try."

After what Valentina assumed was the device changing hands she heard a sonar-like ping. Then the woman said, "See? It just needed a delicate touch!"

"Nothing about you is delicate," the man retorted. "Besides, percussive maintenance is like step two of fixing any technical problem."

"Yes yes, with step one being to ensure it's plugged in. You really need to find a new mantra. That one's getting stale."

"So is this conversation. Hurry up and sweep so we can get strapped in before we dock."

Another ping echoed throughout the corridors outside, this time closer to Valentina's hiding spot. She did her best to cover herself with pressure suits and hold her breath as the pinging got closer and closer. As the device let out a ping right outside the door, she clamped her eyes shut and offered a prayer to any god that would listen. The crew began to jiggle the door lock, only kept out by a piece of metal Valentina had wedged into the mechanism. This was it. She'd been found.

"Damn door's stuck," the man sighed. "And don't even think about telling me percussive maintenance won't fix it this time."

"You can come fix it later on your own then," replied the woman. "But the leak's not in there. It's further up towards the port fuel storage. Come on."

The man gave the storage closet door one final attempt before grumbling and leaving with his companion. Soon Valentina could no longer hear either of their voices or the pinging of the device. Afraid, she blew out through gritted teeth and muttered to herself, "Get it together, Valya. You can't afford to lose it here. Wait until you're off this ship and hopefully moonside. Then you can panic. But not here."

Talking to herself helped, *usually*. The act gave her enough control and focus to unjam the door, grab her two bulging duffle bags, peek out to ensure no one was watching, then steal into the corridors beyond to join the throng of passengers clamoring to get off of the ship as soon as possible. She'd never really experienced such a disgruntled crowd as she did here outside the main airlock that would soon connect the *Arcadia* with the Light Lift's orbital station. They were all tense and complaining while veteran stewardesses attempted to placate them and remind them to hold onto one of the rings in the ceiling above. Valentina easily blended in thanks to her immense desire to be free of the ship. She felt safe enough to watch out of a porthole as the *Arcadia* approached its destination.

Europa was "dirtier" than the holo-vids back on Earth made it out to be. The moon was still an icy, white ball framed by the swirling clouds of Jupiter looming commandingly in the background. But what the holo-vids left out was how cracks and webs of darker colors, mostly rich browns and midnight blacks, broke up the monotonous water-ice crust. Most of them were natural, while a small number were man-made trenches and tunnels that respectively led to Black Ice Mines and down into the moon's ocean. All of the tunnels traced back to the base of the space elevator locked into the ice crust at the equator. The snow-white tower of nanotubes stretched all the way out to space, ending in a torus-shaped space station that was growing closer by the minute.

"First time seeing it for real?"

Valentina twitched slightly as an older gentleman next to her spoke unexpectedly. She turned away from the window to nod at him and say, "Yes. It's far more beautiful than I thought."

Now that she had a good look at him, Valentina could tell this man had seen some time on the ice. His skin was weathered and scarred from repeated exposure, his slightly-sunken, dark eyes sporting crow's feet. But what really cemented this thought was his Ice Hunter outfit. She remembered the Europa-local term for individuals that roamed the frozen tundra in search of mining sites, bounties, and failed expeditions. The thick, jet-black fabric was accented by royal-blue armor pieces, snow-white sleeves, and a fire-orange, furred collar. A patch on his left arm identified him as belonging to the Dusty Winds outfit.

The hunter nodded at the porthole, commenting as they both looked out, "You can always tell who's out here for fun and who's out here to escape. The former are still sitting in their cushy accommodations waiting for the signal to waltz out to whatever tourist trap or resort they've come to experience. The latter, though? They're like you and me: Itching to get out of this cage and onto the true freedom Europa offers."

Valentina clutched the straps of her duffle bags a little tighter. "Maybe I just didn't like the idea of spending more time in that closet."

He laughed, "Heh, maybe. I've had the 'pleasure' of several trips like this, and the *Arcadia* definitely isn't the most spacious of ships to spend a month on. Least it's better than the frozen fleet. It takes a special kind to want to live and work on submarines half the size of this ship. But still, I can tell you're not here to sightsee or cross off some item on a bucket list. It's the way you carry yourself: Jumpy, tense, looking for the next shoe to drop, that sort of thing."

Screaming internally, Valentina gave a nervous laugh and said, " Hah… It's probably just cabin fever…"

The man leaned in, dropping his voice to a level that she had to focus on else risk missing it in the din of the crowd. "Listen, I've been where you are. It's how I started my career as an Ice Hunter over a decade ago. I don't know whether you're planning to go that route or work for a mining corp topside or down in the ocean. But, a word of advice: Don't trust anyone. Out there on the ice the only thing you can trust is your gear and your will to survive. You might look at the Light Lift and think this side of Europa is all glittering rainbows and golden opportunity. The reality is it's all a veneer meant to make the media think we're somehow better than the old wild west."

He paused, leaned back, then continued in a normal voice, "I'd also say that you probably want to dye that hair of yours."

Still processing his sudden advice, Valentina idly ran a hand through her mid-back length, auburn hair. "What's wrong with this color?"

"It identifies you as being an off-worlder," the hunter explained. "Locals, or people wanting to pass as one, all go for whites and platinums. I don't know what or who you're running from, but you probably want to start blending in as soon as possible. Good news is I know one of the stylists at the Frozen Skies Resort here at the station. Just ask for Martha and then tell her that Weinwurm sent you."

Valentina hastily committed those details to memory and began to offer her gratitude, only to be cut off by a sudden shift in gravity as the *Arcadia* came to a stop. She was caught by Weinwurm before she realized she'd nearly fallen over. Her face flushed crimson as she hastily found her feet and offered a simple, "Thanks."

Weinwurm nodded and offered a slight grin, "Don't mention it. One more thing for you to consider as you find your way on Europa. It's a question that an old acquaintance of mine once posed during a night of drinking: *What does a blind man need with an aquarium?* Might seem like a pointless thought experiment at first, but every individual on Europa is affected by it whether they know it or not."

Puzzled, Valentina made a mental note to contemplate that question later. She started to ask what he meant, then the airlock started to cycle and caused the crowd to surge forward before she could get the question out. She lost Weinwurm in all the jostling, though she guessed he wanted to leave the conversation in dramatic fashion. Usually the holo-vids back on Earth depicted Ice Hunters as cutthroat mercenaries that were more concerned about completing their job than their fellow man. Weinwurm's civility and interest in Valentina may have been professional and cold, but his words didn't fit that stereotype.

Valentina disembarked without wasting any time. Similar to airports back on Earth, she walked down a rectangular corridor past two open pressure doors before arriving at the station's main promenade. The first thing she noticed was the faux ceiling. She knew the true ceiling was roughly four stories overhead, yet the carefully synced displays hanging down gave the illusion of an endless, azure sky complete with fluffy, white clouds.

Then came the sheer amount of people moving about. Individuals from all walks of life; be they young dockhands in grease-covered slacks, wrinkled merchants in styles from across the many colonies of the solar system, or high-class tourists in premium furs; journeyed between shops, travel gates, entertainment venues, and resorts that all either connected to or directly opened onto the promenade. A moving walkway took up the center of the "road," with enough distance on either side for a golf cart to travel without having to worry about passersby. Open as the space was, though, the promenade's road notably curved off to the left and right several hundred meters on. Valentina roughly recalled that a full circuit of the promenade was around six kilometers.

The station was, by all rights, a city larger than some back on Earth. One that Valentina hoped she could easily be lost should someone come looking for her. That realization combined with Weinwurm's suggestion in Valentina's mind. The result was she began to notice that nearly all of the shop owners, station workers, resort concierges, food vendors, and more all were sporting hair colors on the frozen end of the color spectrum. Some of the children she saw had notably porcelain-hued cuts. Suddenly Valentina felt like there was a spotlight shining on her. She felt the need to find that resort and this Martha as soon as possible.

In all it only took a glance at a directory and a half-circuit of the promenade to arrive at the Frozen Skies Resort stylized like a mountain lodge - Walls of overlapping, dark wood, windows with fake frosting, and two grand doors with golden knockers shaped like bear skulls. Even the faux sky overhead had been manipulated in conjunction with the atmospheric regulators near the resort to make it look like it was actually snowing. It was the kind of place that Valentina's family might have run back home to capitalize on their majority control over Earth-Luna travel. She tried not to think about that as she slipped inside.

The interior of the resort was just as opulent as the exterior. Furniture made from the same rich wood was carefully positioned around silk carpets and fur rugs. Hunting trophies of beasts from Earth and from Europan xenos hung from the walls, as well as art pieces that Valentina assumed were also a mix of off world and locally sourced. The xenos skulls conjured up mental images of a fierce beast with jaws, horns, and claws capable of turning man and machine alike into scraps. Valentina's eyes moved next to the windows that either opened up to face Europa below or displayed the illusion of a blizzard. To top all of the display off was not one but three different fireplaces with roaring holo-fires.

The concierge desk directly to the left of the door was currently manned by a younger gentleman wearing a crimson suit that matched the accent streaks of red in his otherwise snow-white hair. A marbled-white name tag bearing the name of "Chris" was pinned along with a flower on his right lapel. "Welcome to the Frozen Skies Resort," he said, bowing slightly. "Do you have a reservation?"

Normally, Valentina would have presented a more regal bearing that fit both the atmosphere of the place and her own standing. Yet in a bid to further distance herself from that life, she readjusted the straps of her duffel bags, approached the desk, and answered nervously, "Um, sort of. I'm here to see Martha for her styling services."

Chris raised an eyebrow and straightened his back. "Martha is one of our best spa attendants. If you do not have a reservation you will have to leave your name and a means of contacting you when she is next available. Currently, that is a wait of approximately three months."

Valentina tried not to blanch at that as she hastily replied, "Would it help if I said that Weinwurm sent me?"

The change in Chris' demeanor was like night and day. He went from stiff and all business to relaxed and casual in mere moments. "It would indeed. Mr. Weinwurm often sends promising talents our way. I'd be happy to see you to Martha. Now, if you like."

Amazed at the sudden change, she cautiously questioned, "That's it? No catch?"

He smiled back at her. "No catch. Mr. Weinwurm has provided most of the xenos trophies you see adorning our walls, in addition to those provided by other young stars that he's sent to us. You are, of course, not obliged to do so. We merely ask that you remember us should you chance onto a rare find or spectacular hunt."

"In other words, it's the classic 'scratch my back once you've made it' scenario," Valentina summarized. She was all too familiar with the base idea. It was how her family roped new talent into the business, and pressured them in the form of monetary obligations and quotas. To the point that it treaded the line of legality and organized crime with extreme care. She wasn't getting the same kind of vibe here, though as with everything in her life she approached the situation with paranoid caution. "Very well. Please take me to Martha then."

Chris bowed and moved to escort her throughout the resort. Along the way he made small talk, asking things like how she was adjusting to the reduced gravity and whether her journey here was pleasant. Valentina answered each as basically as possible without giving too many details away. During the walk she noted a grand library, expansive dining room, and a full Earth-normal gravity chamber. Frozen Skies had deep coffers, ones she contributed to by tipping Chris a few credits when they arrived at the spa area. He happily pocketed the coin, spoke a few words to the woman at the desk, bowed, then returned to the front.

The spa was all smooth, pearly, curved walls with recessed floor and ceiling lights. Soothing sounds of snowfall and wind were playing through unseen speakers, along with an artificial breeze blowing throughout the space. As for the receptionist, she was clad in a form-fitting, silver uniform that ended mid-calf. She nodded at Valentina as she rose and motioned for her to follow.

"Right this way, Miss. You've come at a good time. Martha is between appointments at the moment."

Valentina was escorted to a salon chair in the middle of an artificial garden. Small streams filtered through the greenery and along stone channels, providing a pleasant white noise that relaxed her somewhat. A transparent cabinet nearby contained all manner of hair care tools and implements, including some that even she didn't recognize. She pondered the purpose of the tool that looked like a fish hook inverted at the initial curve until Martha arrived.

Martha turned out to be an older woman that moved with the kind of grace that came only with decades of experience. She too was in uniform, though Valentina noted that Martha wore it and not the other way around like with the receptionist. Martha flashed her a smile, then offered in a contralto, "So old 'Wurm found another, eh? He does love his strays. Am I to assume you're wanting to redo your look so you'll blend in a little better?"

Valentina nodded, "Yes, that's right. As you can tell my hair is… Well, it stands out. And that's the last thing I want."

"Simple enough to fix, dear," Martha replied, already in motion towards the cabinet to begin withdrawing tools. "By the time you leave here you'll be an ice princess. But tell me, what brings you to Europa? You don't have to be specific if you don't want to. I can certainly make an educated guess in that instance."

"Am I that obvious?" Valentina wondered aloud. This earned her a laugh from Martha as the older woman started to work on her hair.

"You're not the first rich kid with issues to pass through my door. Some come here to test their skills and see if they can strike it rich a second time. Others want to experience frontier life and see if the grass is greener on the other side of the fence. And then there's those that journey out this far because they're running from something or someone. I'm betting you're in the latter group."

Part of Valentina wanted to let the comment pass in awkward silence. Yet it felt rude considering she was essentially getting this service for free. She ended up relenting, though not fully, "Let's just say that I was supposed to get married to the wrong kind of guy. And the only way to not go through with it was to come out to Europa."

Martha worked and hummed for a bit before commenting, "Must be a pretty rotten fellow to warrant giving up friends, family, and whatever else you had back home."

"You could say that," replied Valentina as her thoughts turned to Rolf Wesler and her abode back on Earth. "He's the ruthless type that wanted a trophy wife that would bow to his every whim. Which meant that someone like me who had been living in a gilded cage her whole life was a perfect candidate."

"Mhm. Mhm. Yet here you are, rebelling against that. And I'm willing to bet it's not the first time you've tried something like this."

"This is attempt four or five," Valentina admitted. "Though this one has definitely worked out much better."

Martha continued her efforts on both hair and conversation without even the slightest pause, "Seems like it, if you're here. Any idea what you'll end up doing on Europa? Stay up here in the Light Station? Head down to the surface? Go below the ice to one of the oceanic settlements?"

Valentina recalled a popular band of Ice Hunters that had shown up frequently in Earth media. "I was sort of hoping I could sign up to be an Ice Hunter with the Sisters of Solace. But I don't have anywhere near enough experience to become one right out of the gate."

"Hah, aiming for the sky I see! I don't understand why they have such high entry requirements. Especially that condition that you had to bring in a bounty worth more than a thousand credits without using a gun or any restraints. Seems like a recipe for disaster."

"It probably is. Which is why I'm probably going to try signing up with a mining corp on the surface. It'll give me experience and credits to boot. Then maybe once I feel I have enough skill I'll try to join the Sisters."

"I see. I see. Well, you're all done, dear. Take a look." Martha produced a mirror and showed Valentina her new look. Overall, her hair was now diamond dust, with a few defining streaks of pitch-black here and there. "I don't know where you're headed after this, but I tried to give you one of the trendy colorings going around lately."

"It looks great," replied Valentina earnestly. "Thank you."

"Don't mention it. Oh, and if you see old 'Wurm again tell him he owes me that drink."

CHAPTER 2
Owen - Blue Bison Mining Site, Alagonian Depths

Deep below the ice, in the vast, dark oceans of Europa, a web of pinpricks of light expanded as alpha shift began for the Blue Bison Mining Consortium. Drones and divers equipped with vibration drills flowed down from their holding pens aboard the command and control (C&C) submarine, the *E.S.V. Sequana*, towards vast deposits of Gadolinium and Black Ice on the ocean floor. Other remotely-operated vehicles traveled perpendicular to the *Sequana* to establish an outer ring of lights. A boundary that kept the mining teams safe from the indigenous wildlife, known as rhadas by all but off-worlders, as they worked. This particular site was well established, though there was always a chance of a rhadas incursion. A fact not lost on Owen Jones, who had lost his father to an attack.

That was over nine years ago. Now 19, Owen worked for the same company his father had. He was one of many divers that supervised and maintained the drilling drones as they worked. Their shifts consisted of standing or floating around while waiting for something to break or jam. Which meant that Owen and the rest of the divers had plenty of time to chatter and get lost in their thoughts. Today saw him zoning out within his pressure suit until something bumped into him. Startled, he wheeled around and instantly felt the blood drain from his face.

Floating behind him was an open eye over five stories tall. An alien eye with three pupils, each larger than Owen, arranged in a triangular fashion that glowed crimson with bioluminescence bright enough to cause him to squint. This eye belonged to only one type of local creature: A Leviathan. A creature so large, powerful, and deadly that even a whole fleet of attack craft would be hard-pressed to injure it. Leviathans had killed Owen's father, and were seen as the scourge and devil of all ocean life.

Panic overtook Owen. He backpedaled, screaming while waving his technician's toolkit before him like a weapon. His right heel slammed into something and sent him falling over backwards. A loud crunch marked his contact with the ocean floor. Gravity may have only been a seventh of Earth-normal, but it was enough of an impact to knock the wind out of him. His vision swirled to inky darkness as he pitched upwards towards the ice miles above and waited for the Leviathan to end it all.

It never came. Instead, another diver's helmet popped into view as they leaned over Owen's head. "Easy there, kid! Relax!"

The voice belonged to Isaac Hall, Owen's shift leader, a source of comfort and respect for Owen. Enough that he was able to get control of his breathing and cease flailing about wildly. Then, when Isaac offered out a hand, Owen readily took it, stood once more, and looked about. There was no Leviathan. Not so much a flicker of light on the outer defensive ring.

"What the hell happened, kid?" Isaac asked, concern apparent in his voice. "One moment you were quiet on comms and the next you were blowing out everyone's ears."

Owen replied after taking a deep, shuddering breath, "Just my mind playing tricks on me, boss. Thought a Leviathan had somehow snuck up on me."

"Happens to the best of us, lad. Take the rest of alpha shift off. Rest, decompress, and process."

"I'm alright now," Owen insisted. "I can keep working."

Though the actual faceplate of their helmets were both opaque when looking outside-in, Owen pictured Isaac shaking his head with a frown. "Nah. This is the first time it's ever happened to you. On this scale, anyways. I'm not going to risk it. Take the R&R to decompress and process. If you really want to make up your lost hours then come back towards the rear end of gamma shift."

Owen considered protesting but knew it wouldn't get him anywhere. As he deflated, he responded, "You're right, boss. I'll go back to the *Sequana* for now. Won't happen again."

Isaac drew an upwards arc over his opaque helmet, symbolizing a smile. Then he swam off to check on the drone that Owen had been overseeing moments ago. Owen began the journey back to the *E.S.V. Sequana*. Along the way he kicked himself despite knowing that he wasn't to blame for anything that happened.

The truth was that everyone that lived in the Sea of Sarpedon accepted the fact that their lives could end in a mere instant from a Leviathan attack, a pressure seal breaking, or a loss of oxygen. The list of ways one could die stretched on and on. When this list combined with the ever-present, ominous darkness and long work hours the fact was that sometimes people just broke. Even veteran miners could experience the same kind of episode that Owen just had without any warning. It's why there was such a high attrition rate among miners, and why most ocean-dwellers rotated surface-side in their late twenties. If not earlier.

Still, Owen felt he let the rest of his team down. Doubly so when he checked his chronometer and saw that it was barely 0245, a mere three hours into his first 14-hour shift. The way shifts tended to work for mining operations like this was 14 hours on and 28 hours off rotation between three teams. Two full rotations accounted for what was considered a "day" on Europa, a total of 84 hours back on Earth. And while Owen didn't have to come back for part of gamma shift to make up for his lost hours, he felt an immense obligation and social pressure to do so despite the risk of straining himself further. Everyone worked their hardest down in these depths despite the risks to both mind and body. Individuals down here either were chasing a lofty credit payout so they could retire early, or they had nowhere else to go. As a result, idleness and laziness were something that ocean-dweller culture shunned. Or so had been drilled into Owen since his arrival at Europa ten years ago with his father. He'd lived and breathed the miner lifestyle for the important portion of his formative years.

Thoughts like these plagued Owen as he got closer to the *Sequana*. It only had running lights to the naked eye, but to his pressure suit's enhanced sensors, it was a beacon of light against the encroaching darkness. Floating pretty at 542 meters long, 182 meters at its widest, and 118 meters tall, the stadium-shaped *Sequana* was the heart of not just the mining operation but also a mobile community. Over a thousand individuals called it home, of all vocations and walks of life. It could self-sustain for up to four months, more if it was being constantly supplied by transport vessels that exchanged necessities for the precious Gadolinium and Black Ice that was mined.

Two transport vessels were currently docked with the *Sequana* in a remora-like manner. The transports' escorts, three *Thalassa*-class attack variants, lingered nearby with the two *Thalassa* assigned to protect the *Sequana*, the *E.S.V. Abalone* and the *Anemone*. Each of the attack submarines were designed in sleek, sloping curves that allowed them to dart and twist through the water at surprising speeds. Their crews were barely forty in number, yet their firepower was significant. With guided torpedoes, sonic weaponry, and grappler arms, the *Thalassa* could handle nearly any threat while running circles around their prey. Though when faced with a Leviathan all bets were off.

All these moving parts and vehicles necessitated that Owen take a controlled, regulated approach. He let his suit and the automated traffic control systems aboard the *Sequana* handle most of the work. There were actual, human controllers monitoring everything, but logistics like this were best left to the computer core that was capable of over 10 trillion operations per second. A common joke/hope among ocean-dwellers was that one day robots would completely take over mining operations like this, leaving humans to sit safely in control rooms of facilities anchored to the ice crust ceiling above. But there were a few "die-hard" types that swore they'd never let a machine replace them. Owen knew of a couple himself, though only by name and reputation.

After swimming into a designated airlock on the side of the *Sequana* with several other divers, Owen cycled into the ship proper. Thirty minutes passed as he divested himself from his pressure suit and stowed it properly in his designated alcove/locker. Then came a quick shower and replacing his sweat-soaked under suit with a set of loose-fitting, comfortable layers of clothes that kept the frigid air of the submarine at bay. The vessel may have been a wonder of technology, but the *Sequana* couldn't afford to keep the ambient temperature higher than 6° C outside of the mess hall and officer's quarters. Overall, an atmosphere great for sleeping under heavy blankets, but not pleasant to wander around in otherwise.

Regardless, Owen was now left wondering what to do. The adrenalin still pumping through his veins kept him from revisiting his hallucination, but that could change any minute. When it did, he'd have to confront what had happened and come to terms with it. That he'd suffered his first real break seemingly out of the blue with no triggers. Sure, he still sometimes thought he could see the "running lights" of the rhadas looming beyond the protective drone barrier as he worked. And now and again he'd feel sudden dread for no real reason. But those two things were considered normal for ocean-dwellers. Hallucinating a full-on Leviathan was a troubling sign of mental degradation.

A few potential fixes came to mind for Owen. A tempting one involved visiting Red Deck and spending some of his hard-earned credits on enough booze and sex to wash the memories from his mind. Another involved catching whatever the latest holo-flick from Earth was. What won the day was Owen traveling to one of the virtual reality (VR) suites aboard the *Sequana* to engage in a program he'd run at least once a week since his father's death.

Owen's lucky timing got him into a VR suite within the hour instead of having to wait. The suite was a three-meter, matte-gray cube featuring floors that would move with the user, body trackers for haptic feedback, one of the best sound systems in the solar system, and a full-immersion headset was anchored to the ceiling above. After strapping all the trackers on and slipping the headset over his head, Owen wasn't in the depths of Europa's oceans any more. He was next to a large oak tree in the middle of an endless sea of grass and flowers. Light wind played across his ears as a holographic menu of sharp lines and ephemeral text projected in front of him.

This was just the lobby. The actual program Owen had come here to experience was one he'd cobbled together and modified over the years. One far less pleasant of an environment than his current surroundings. After a few swipes and an access code the world swirled around him into something that couldn't be more different.

He was now "floating" as a *Thalassa*-class, just how tactical officers used their VR suites to "become" the submarine and act in real time against a threat. He could see where his "body" began and ended in the watery void along with readouts similar to his pressure suit. Unlike his pressure suit, though, there were weapon controls: Sonic blasts for the smaller rhadas and any hostile divers, as well as torpedoes for medium rhadas and enemy subs. But he wouldn't be using either in this program. Instead, he'd rely on the type of weapon normally reserved as a last resort, as an emergency cutting tool, or as a dueling implement: Vibrochainsaws.

Every vessel, even the mighty *Sequana*, had at least two fully-articulated arms that bore these massive instruments of destruction. They were flush with the hull when stowed, which meant deploying them was quite the spectacle. One that could easily scare off both rhadas and pirates alike. Especially when the *Thalassa*-class flared out six lengths of glowing, metallic-orange death.

The grappling arms were a weapon that had become synonymous with the Sea of Sarpedon, the underwater frontier of Europa, much like how revolvers were linked with the Old West on Earth. But this program wasn't a virtual dueling match between two subs. Instead, it was something that every ocean-dweller indulged in from time to time: a survival gauntlet against rhadas. Unlike the normal programs, though, Owen's was a specific scenario.

The program started simple: a series of smaller rhadas began to swarm around Owen's virtual submarine, gnashing out with tentacles and teeth powerful enough to leave dents and scratches on the hull. Again, in a normal program, these would be the tutorial enemies, meant to test the haptic feedback and get the user familiar with the controls. However, in Owen's, he actually felt pinpricks of induced pain as if the virtual avatar was his own body. Masochistic, perhaps, but a necessary step as far as Owen was concerned. After all, actual tactical officers in real combat felt the same things in their VR suites. This wasn't just a mindless game. Not anymore. The safeties were on in this VR suite, but despite their dampening a great deal of simulated injury reached Owen. This was the closest Owen could get to the real thing. Near-real was required if he was going to relive *that* day once more.

After slicing apart the smaller rhadas swarm with his vibrochainsaws, Owen began to dance with a horde of larger creatures. Their designs were truly alien - somewhere between a giant squid mixed with a great white shark that had an affair with an eel. They offered more of a challenge and more of a combat high with each and every weathered blow. Enough that Owen lost two arms and a quarter of movement speed before he eliminated them.

Then came the next wave, and the next. The simulation was an impossible battle against impossible odds. Yet, Owen persisted. Long enough to see the "end" of the program. An end marked by the arrival of a Leviathan. Owen's goal had always been to make it to the end with enough vibrochainsaws intact to destroy the rhadas that had killed his father. But by this point all he had was a barely-intact rudder and an 80% compromised hull. He could do nothing but scream at the creature as it opened its fathomless jaws wide and ate Owen.

That was where the program ended. Owen was returned to the tree and the field, panting and covered in real sweat. It was at that moment that he realized why his break earlier in the day was bothering him so much. He'd finally lost control of his inner demons and could no longer keep them contained in VR. That scared him, but not as much as the triple-pupiled eye that met his own eyes when he looked up.

"You're not fucking real!" he bellowed, tearing off his headset in fear and returning fully to reality. The matte-gray cube was silent save for his labored breathing.

Owen wondered if he still could still manage to spend some time in the bars of Red Deck getting plastered before he had to hit the racks for sleep.

CHAPTER 3

Thatch - E.F.S.V. Wolffish, Minos Mire

"Damage report, Mr. Yukawa?"

"Green across the board, Admiral!"

"Good. Status of the convoy, Ms. Volodina?"

"They're already transmitting the white flag."

Admiral Amaya Thatch rose from her skull-inlaid chair, moved over to the communications station, and motioned for Volodina to hand her the microphone. Once in hand, Thatch keyed up and proclaimed, "Alright, boys, here's how we're going to proceed. We're taking your cargo but not your lives or your subs, so long as you don't do anything stupid. If you DO decide to try something funny... Well, I'm sure you've heard the tales of what happens when people cross me. And if you haven't, you'd best pray you never have to find out first hand. My first mate will be in touch with you shortly."

She tossed the mic to Yukawa with a wink. "Go easy on them. Make it seem like we can't fit all their cargo so they get to keep some of it. Then give them the usual line about how lucky they were that I was in a good mood."

Yukawa plucked the mic out of the air with a thrust faster than that of a master fencer. He might have actually had been a fencer in a past life for all Thatch knew. She'd never gotten around to asking despite him being her first mate for over five years now. It just hadn't come up. Though maybe he'd ask him later at dinner in the mess hall.

"You got it, Admiral," he confirmed. "Same orders as usual if they put up a fuss?"

Thatch ran a hand through her hair and then flared it out dramatically. "They heard me just now. They've been warned appropriately. But in the event they're bigger idiots than they were coming into my waters to begin with, let's keep the headcount low, say… 10%?"

"Understood."

Thatch turned to nod at Volodina, "Work your magic and coordinate everything as Yukawa asks. If you need me, I'll be in my ready room."

Volodina smiled warmly, as she always did when given a direct order that she knew she could handle. "Got it, Cap'n!"

After patting the woman's shoulder twice, Thatch exited the bridge of her C&C submarine, the *E.F.S.V. Wolffish*, and moved into her stateroom. It was modestly designed for an Admiral of her station, with enough space to entertain a guest or two while also fitting a queen-sized bed with rose-red linens, a dark oak desk, and a refresher unit that only worked properly if kicked twice before use. The walls bore trophies that Thatch had collected over the years, ranging from actual xenos skulls to literal hats that had once belonged to notable submarine captains she'd defeated. The desk had both a private terminal and a small terrarium containing cryptanthus and rich soil from Earth.

As Admiral of the Dread Lurkers, Thatch was in charge of over fifteen vessels and three or more concurrent operations at any given point in time. Most of the operations were guerilla mining sorties in the Minos Mire. Established mining sites in the ocean of the Light Side of Europa, the Alagonian Depths, had the luxury of force projection and enough firepower to handle most rhadas incursions. These impromptu operations on the Dark Side's ocean, the Minos Mire, had no such things. Their aim was to fill cargo holds as fast as possible before the ferocity of the rhadas attacks forced a retreat. Dangerous and risky, but damned profitable.

Currently there were two such mining endeavors taking place that necessitated Thatch's attention. One had begun not two hours ago, while the second was getting towards the end of the operational window. She keyed up a channel towards the captain in charge and was face to face with a heavily-scarred man older than her.

"How's the drilling going, O'Dea?" Thatch asked with a smirk. "You're staying longer than you usually do."

O'Dea let out a huff and crossed his arms. "Trust me, I wanted to be out of here two hours ago after one of the boys thought he spotted a Leviathan in the distance. But apparently the Black Ice in this deposit is premium shit. We gotta get as much as possible because we're not going to be able to come back for months. Least, judging how bad the rhadas keep assaulting us."

O'Dea's reasoning made perfect sense to Thatch. After all, Black Ice was the most profitable export from Europa, to the point that it was more valuable than gold back in the old west. This was thanks to induction thermal plasma methods that could convert the material into hydrogen and carbon nanotubes. The hydrogen made for premium fuel, and the nanotubes were utilized in ship construction of all varieties. Both in such high demand to risk not just coming to Europa's deadly oceans but also drilling without much backup.

"I trust your judgment," Thatch replied firmly. "If you think you can manage it, then stay. Else bug out and head back to the Dark Lift. You're no use to me dead. Nor would the Black Ice serve anyone any good sitting in a sub carcass at the bottom of the ocean."

"Yeah yeah. How'd the convoy raid go?" asked O'Dea.

"Better than expected. Only had to fire off two warning torpedoes before they got the message. I've got Yukawa handling the finer details."

"Hah! You need to give in and hand that kid his own command already. Or at least cut him a bigger share."

Still smirking, Thatch raised an eyebrow as she answered, "Just like how I have to keep adjusting your take? Rich as we are, I can't have both you and Yukawa at Captain level. You'd get into bidding wars and end up turning on each other."

O'Dea shrugged, rubbing his right forearm. "Well, you gotta keep him loyal somehow."

"Is it really that hard for you to believe he might simply be loyal because he actually is, instead of loyal thanks to how much I pay and reward him?"

The lights behind O'Dea flickered as he lurched to the right. "Look, all I'm saying is money and power is how you keep kids like that from getting uppity."

"Uppity enough to take over the entire operation, you mean? Like I did to you?"

O'Dea lurched once more on the screen. Clearly things were ramping up on his end. "Call it what you want. I also *gave* you command because it was my time to step down."

"Uh huh. Well, I'm guessing with all the bouncing around you're doing on screen that things are getting rough for you. Wrap up your cycle and get out of there," ordered Thatch.

"If you insist," he relented, though not with enough conviction to make her believe he wasn't relieved for an excuse to leave. "See you back at the Dark Lift."

Thatch's terminal screen winked as the call ended. She was now presented with enough graphs, spreadsheets, and projections that could make an experienced accountant's head spin. The takeaway was that the Dread Lurkers were firmly in the green. Even the purchase of another *Namaka*-class fast attack raider hadn't been too costly. The Dread Lurkers weren't the richest band of pirates on the dark side of Europa, but they definitely made enough to be respectable.

Respect came with a certain level of safety. At least from other rogues and mercenaries. Europa's local aquatic denizens didn't care who you were or what you were sailing in. Especially if you were disturbing a hydrothermal vent or resource deposit. The Dark Side of Europa played by different rules than the light side. Rhadas attacks were more frequent and more violent no matter where in the Minos Mire you were. Death by Leviathan was just as likely as getting stabbed in the back by someone on your crew. It all depended on luck, how observant you were, and what vibroknife you had hidden.

Everything about the numbers seemed to check out to Thatch's trained eyes. A few people in her organization were grifting off the top, but she always kept those numbers within acceptable boundaries. She'd learned from the best, after all - A mentor that drilled into her that it was better to be magnanimous than to rule with an iron fist and with fear. People on Europa had enough to be fearful of. Why make things worse for them?

A chime at her door interrupted her number-crunching. "Enter," she ordered at the door.

Yukawa stepped in with a slight bow. Immediately Thatch could tell something was wrong. One hand wandered to her right leg out of caution as she calmly asked, "What's up, first mate?"

"It's about the convoy, Admiral. I... Er..."

"Spit it out."

He winced as he briefly explained, "They didn't make it."

"Explain," Thatch commanded, still in a level, pleasant tone.

"According to long range sensors, a Leviathan got 'em twenty minutes after we turned them loose."

"And you expect me to be angry about that?"

"Well... er... you did say only 10% casualties were acceptable..."

Thatch sighed, rose from her desk, and moved to place a calming hand on Yukawa's shoulder. "That's true. I only wanted us to be the reason for that 10%. But if a Leviathan came swimming up and ate them, that's not our problem. They should have run dark for longer instead of what I'm assuming was full flank speed away from us. Did you warn them before you left?"

"I did, yes," Yukawa confirmed, relaxing somewhat.

"Then you did all you could. It's just a shame that we didn't take all their cargo. Now part of it's sitting in a Leviathan's stomach. But this isn't like you, Yukawa. You've seen this sort of thing happen before. What makes this one different?"

He hesitated, drawing out a pregnant pause before answering, "One of the crew over there looked like my sister."

Things began to click in Thatch's mind. "It's been three years since you lost her, yes? It's only natural for you to feel at odds if someone similar looking popped up."

"Maybe, Ma'am. But it got me thinking about the argument I had with my sis before she left that day. About how we left things angry and how I never got the chance to apologize. Now I've gone and sent her stunt double to the same fate. I must be cursed."

Evident turmoil played across Yukawa's face. Thatch sighed, removed her hand from his shoulder, and told him, "Whoever you saw wasn't her, first mate. It's not your fault. You aren't 'cursed'. Everyone down here in the Sea of Sarpedon knows the end could come at any moment. It's why it's so easy for a crew to bond and feel like family after only a short period of time. That family, real or otherwise, constantly changes. The key is not getting caught up in the loss or in trying to play catch up. You'll only burn yourself out that way. And then you'd be something worse than Leviathan food: You'd be alone."

Though her words didn't fully alleviate his worries, Thatch could tell they broke Yukawa's spiraling thoughts. This was confirmed when he forced a weak smile in saying, "Yeah, you got a point, Admiral. Sorry to bother you with this. The good news is they had some choice gadolinium in their holds. We got enough of it to maybe rival O'Dea's spoils this time out."

"That's what I like to hear. And don't feel as if you're burdening me with stuff like this. I'd much rather play counselor if it means keeping a reliable first mate on hand."

That was enough for that weak smile on Yukawa's face to become a genuine grin. "Thanks, Ma'am. I'll return to cataloging our loot. ETA to the Dark Lift is about two days."

"Carry on then."

Thatch remained in place until the door sealed shut, then she let out a great sigh. If she had a credit for every time she'd dealt with a conversation like that, she'd be richer than the orbital barons of Mars.

CHAPTER 4
Valentina - Light Lift

Valentina's trip down the Light Lift was going better than expected. No one spared her a second glance, nor bothered her with conversation, after she left the Frozen Skies Resort. She obtained a lift pass with little ceremony, and in the process she scored a seat near the windows of the space elevator. The spectacular expanse of Europa's frozen surface rose to meet Valentina as the lift descended, reminding her of a ski trip she once took to the Swiss Alps back on Earth. Though unlike that trip there was the orange globe of Jupiter filling the horizon against a backdrop of countless stars.

A tour group of socialites was seated behind Valentina. They reminded her of that same ski trip in how some of the noble born thought their money could buy them gear that would make up for a lack of skill. In other words, a peacock display of wealth. The group's tour guide was similarly a high-value sherpa that was happily rattling off facts about the Light Lift and Europa:

"...the initial drilling for the Lift's anchors took roughly six months, followed by an assembly process that took almost two years to complete. The end result is the same car you're currently in. It completes a full cycle every 26 hours, with an hour reserved for actual transit between either end. Most of the time the lift is being loaded/unloaded with as much goods as it can safely hold. Those shipments that do not qualify for Lift use, or require a faster time table, have to be taken up using actual landing craft."

One of the women in the tour group with a voice as shrill as her copious jewelry was distracting asked, "What about shipments from the ocean? Does the Lift go all the way down?"

The tour guide answered without missing a beat, "The actual space elevator terminates at the surface. However, a secondary elevator between the surface and the ocean ten miles below is situated right below it. It's designed more for cargo and subnautical vehicles than passengers, and cycles roughly every 44 hours. There are other routes to and from the ocean via a network of tunnels, with travel times ranging from 48 to 96 hours depending on congestion and vehicle type."

Another tourist spoke up, this time a man with a soothing vibrato, "Why is it called the 'Light Lift' exactly? Is there such a thing as the 'Dark Lift?'"

"Indeed, there is! To explain, the moon of Europa is gravity-locked such that the same side always faces Jupiter. The side that faces away from the planet is colloquially referred to as the 'Light Side,' and the side that faces towards Jupiter the 'Dark Side.' The Dark Side does receive some sunlight during Europa's three-and-a-half-day orbit around Jupiter, but for the most part is cloaked in darkness. Hence the name.

"As for the Dark Lift, it's generally viewed as a dangerous venture not worth the risk. Not just because of the dangers that come with perpetual darkness, but also the risky burns spaceships have to take in order to dock with the connected station. To say nothing of the ruthless pirates, mercenaries, and other vagabonds that call the place home. Or how vicious the local wildlife is on that side of the moon. But let's not focus on that! You came here to climb the Singate Massif. It's one of the largest isolated mountains of the Carnus Expanse, and reasonably close to the Light Lift…"

Valentina tuned out as the tour guide's monologue switched away from topics relevant to her. Instead, she spent the rest of the ride down to the surface confirming the details of her appointment. She was to meet with a representative of the Midnight Hearts Mining Company at their offices at the base of the Light Lift an hour after arriving. Assuming she passed muster, she would begin training immediately, followed by being taken out to one of the company's mining sites. It wasn't likely she would have to work with Black Ice due to its scarcity on the surface. Instead, she would probably be involved in Gadolinium extraction. Surface deposits weren't nearly as rich as those in the ocean, yet there was still enough of the element to warrant actual mining operations.

The lift slowed as it approached its terrestrial berth. Out of the window Valentina could see a frozen cityscape that spiraled out from the lift. All of the buildings had tubes connecting them to one another without exposing travelers to the elements. Only on the outskirts of the settlement could vehicles be seen. Most of the vehicles were entering and leaving from tunnels that went not just beneath the city but also stretched down to the ocean (if the tour guide was to be believed). What mattered to her was somewhere in the iced-over spires was her ticket to further freedom and hopefully cementing her escape from home.

Walls soon filled the viewports of the lift before it finally touched down. Valentina was one of the first ones off, eager to get on with her plan. The terminal area was similar to that of the station above in that the base of the Light Lift felt like an underground mall that stretched on forever. However, after obtaining directions and setting on her way, that illusion was dispelled by the emergence of actual windows. She didn't feel like she was trapped, despite briefly feeling so on the station.

Valentina's shoulders relaxed from the stiff state she'd been holding since leaving the salon. Her fear of being caught, sent back, and the horrors that entailed held her tighter than the grip of a free climber. Especially when she noticed that the tour group from before was headed in the same direction as her. They were loud, obnoxious. The type of rich idiot that thought hearing their own voice was heavenly and others should leap at the chance to sample it. Combined with their designer gear and their out-of-place hair colors, they were the brightest peacocks at the ball. They reminded Valentina of several nobles back on Earth that actively competed for everyone's attention at parties, including Wesler. That line of thought soured her view and made her wish she wouldn't have to tolerate them much longer.

The good news was that the tour group veered off as Valentina took a side passage up an escalator. Once their peacocking was no longer audible, she let out a held breath and tried to focus on getting to her destination. The escalator let her out onto one of the bands of multiple moving walkways that filled the tubes connecting the settlement together. Hoping between them like one would change lanes on a highway, Valentina took an "exit" that saw the ceiling open up as the moving walkway reached its conclusion at one of the domes where the Midnight Heart offices were located. Most of the space in the dome was a gigantic warehouse in which vehicles were being serviced, shipments entered the logistical chain, and various training pods were in use. The actual office space consisted of a two story, matte-gray, rectangular building that felt more like an afterthought - A temporary installment rather than a permanent office. Though once inside she had to reconsider that notion. The decorations couldn't compare to those of the Frozen Skies Resort, but the multitude of paintings, holo-displays, and glass-encased rare minerals were impressive enough that Valentina could tell actual thought and credits had gone into their arrangement.

After a brief conversation with the receptionist (in which Valentina gave her false name of "Sarah") and five minutes of waiting, she was sitting face to face with one of the company recruiters in a small conference room. The bags under his eyes suggested that sleep was a luxury he could not afford. That and how much coffee he consumed from a thermos as they talked.

"Right, so, Sarah, why do you want to come work for us?" he asked after introducing himself as Thomas. "We'll certainly take what help we can get, but you don't give me the impression that you've ever done work like this before. Usually, pretty faces like yours stay up in space or in the penthouses down here."

The casual pass at her brought forth stomach-flipping anxiety as Valentina forced away a memory of Wesler. After pushing down her revulsion, she relied on one of the lines she had practiced countless times in her head, "It's important that I get hands-on experience with surviving and working out on the ice. Otherwise, I cannot join the Sisters of Solace one day."

"Oh? I suppose that explains some things then. Though I will be blunt and tell you that it's not going to be a cakewalk. You're going to be pushed to your limit nearly every day. Many aspiring miners wash out before training is complete. And fewer still actually see time on the ice proper. The surface isn't as deadly as the oceans are, but we still try to limit the danger we put people in. It could end up that we shuffle you into a position that doesn't contribute to the goal you're pursuing. So, with all that in mind, are you still sure you want to sign up?"

A few moments of hesitation were all Valentina needed to cement her conviction. "Even if I do 'wash out' as you say, I'll still be gaining valuable skills and knowledge. I came to Europa to escape the cushy life, not end up right back in it. I may not look like much now, but I promise I can contribute my fair share and give a hundred percent."

Thomas chuckled back, "Eh, you can scale it back to seventy-five-ish percent. We don't like burning workers out, especially considering how much time, effort, and credits goes into training them. Now that said, you would essentially have to sign a contract stipulating that your first two months of pay would go to paying back the company for such training, in addition to the standard issue equipment that you'll be provided. After that you will be paid out every other week with bonuses for performance. You alright with that?"

"Perfectly."

"Good. Here's the forms you'll need to sign."

After reading the contract carefully, Valentina signed off as "Sarah" before pushing the forms back across the table towards Thomas. "There we are. So where do I begin now?"

Thomas briefly checked the forms before answering, "First things first, you'll be attending classes on survival and equipment operation/repair. Pass those and you get to start learning in VR. Pass *that* you then get to move up to the full-sim pods. And then at the end of all that you get to go out to one of the mining sites. Should take roughly a month, starting tomorrow. You actually came at a great time. One day later and you would have needed to wait another two weeks before the next round of training started."

"Maybe I'm just lucky then," she offered with a slight smirk, even if she didn't feel that was the case despite how much she had practiced her facade. Aside from the whole hair business, everything was proceeding according to her original plan. Though Valentina still had to reassure herself that this time her escape would work and that it wouldn't all end up with her back on a transport to Earth with Wesler.

"Eh, don't count your rhadas quite yet. The ice is a cruel mistress. As are our instructors. Survive the first week and then you can start thinking about luck again."

CHAPTER 5

Owen - Blue Bison Mining Site, Alagonian Depths

A week had passed since Owen experienced the Leviathan hallucination. Life returned to normal, or about as normal as living and working in Europa's ocean could be. He woke up, showered, slipped into his dive suit, worked for a full shift, hung up his dive suit, showered again, then caught some sleep before the next alpha shift to repeat the process over again. Frivolities were kept to a minimum, even his visits to the VR suites. Owen made up his lost work hours and tried to perform at 110% of what was required of him. This pleased his supervisor, but Owen picked up on the fact that Isaac was keeping him on a shorter leash. For one, his work assignments were farther from the defensive net and closer to the *Sequana*. He also wasn't drilling Black Ice. Gadolinium was technically safer to mine, but it was the same sort of difference between an apple and an orange at the end of the day. Owen suspected that Isaac was trying to gauge if he could handle the same pressure as before. The perceived judgment was both welcome and annoying.

This all meant that Owen was paying more attention to the comms chatter between his teammates throughout his shift. Today's inane debate was between Edmond and Marcus about the roleplaying game they indulged in every couple of days. Hobbies like that were an important pastime for those that couldn't afford or wrangle VR Suite time. That made the participants all the more passionate about their hobby, to the point that neither Edmond nor Marcus was giving the other ground.

"I'm telling you, Marcus, there isn't a right way to go about it. No matter what you do, you're just going to cause waves for everyone involved," came the perpetually-tired-sounding voice of the German-born Edmond.

The dulcet tones of Marcus replied, "Edmond, listen, I'm not going to poison a whole year's worth of work just because Thompson can't keep it in his pants. I made it very clear at the beginning of the campaign that there wouldn't be any explicit romance scenes, especially intra-party ones."

"Yeah, well, if you do go and kick Thompson out, what's that do for your story? Aren't you going to have to basically rewrite the entire back half of the campaign?"

"I'd rather do that than listen to Thompson trying to hit on Anna both in and out of character. Seriously, I get that it's meant to be escapism and that working down here fucks with everyone. But there's a point where I need to put my foot down as gamemaster. I've given him ample warning and plenty of opportunities to change his behavior."

Edmond sighed in resignation, "Guess there's no shortage of replacement players you can pull from. But hell, I just see this all coming back to bite us in the ass somehow. Beta shift already are a bunch of tossers. This would just add fuel to that fire. Ain't that right, Squeeze?"

Owen grumbled as he keyed up his mic in response to hearing his nickname, "Maybe if you hadn't slept with and then ghosted half of beta shift you wouldn't feel like they're a problem." That got a laugh from everyone listening in.

Edmond included as he retorted at Owen, "Not all of us can get what we need from VR suites, Squeeze. Some of us need the real, physical warmth and touch of another human being. Not my fault if the people I sleep with can't hold a morning-after conversation. If they wanted to be more than friends with benefits then they should at least put in effort to further such a relationship. Can't always be me taking the initiative." Edmond retorted.

Before Marcus came to Owen's defense a loud ping echoed through the waters of the mining site. Almost everyone turned towards the indicator in their helmet's display that highlighted the defensive drone that had gone active. An injured rhadas the size of a micro-torpedo was slinking away back towards a small swarm of its fellows. This prompted a few more rhadas to try to get past the drone to no avail. The shockwave from the drone's sound-based weaponry was more than enough to cripple creatures of that size. The fact such an assault was happening during alpha shift was concerning. Usually, gamma shift got the worst of rhadas attacks, with alpha being the calm after the battle.

"Stay focused, folks," came Isaac's authoritative voice over the comms. "It's just a school of the bastards. Nothing to be alarmed about. Scouting parties and the *Sequana*'s sensors aren't picking up any major movements in the surrounding area. You'll be the first to know if I hear otherwise."

With that alpha shift (Owen included) returned to their jobs. However, in Owen's case, something glinting caused him to stop his mining drone's vibrodrill. He moved to get a better look at it as whatever it was once again put out a burst of gamma radiation. Nothing down this deep should have been putting off that kind of radiation. The good news was that the bursts were not hazardous to his health, though they still warranted a more in-depth investigation. As his helmet swept up and down the electromagnetic spectrum, Owen saw that the uncovered object was a part of a prolate spheroid. The object's surface was impossibly smooth, making it easy to pick the mystery item out of the surrounding Gadolinium ore chunks even without the gamma bursts.

"The hell are you?" he said, reaching out to touch it. Whatever it was it would have to be removed before his drone could resume drilling to mitigate any chance of damage. And as far as his pressure suit could tell it was safe enough to handle.

That notion changed when Owen's gauntlet made contact. A jolt of energy surged through his suit and up his arm. His ears rang and his vision narrowed as he wrenched his hand back to cut off the flow of the lightning. The entire left side of his body tingled and his head ached worse than any hangover-induced migraine he'd ever experienced. And when his vision properly returned, the object had disappeared. His suit's sensors could find no trace of whatever it had been. There wasn't so much as a thumb-sized void in the Gadolinium where he had found the object.

Another hallucination perhaps? Owen thought.

"Everything alright over there, Owen?" Isaac asked in Owen's ear. "Your heart rate just shot up."

Owen gritted his teeth through the pain in his temples and forced himself to lie in an attempt to salvage his forward progress this week, "Nothing to worry about. I thought I'd lost my gravivariable wrench when fixing my drone. Found it though so we're good."

Isaac's tone was polite, but with a slight air of authority that one usually reserved for when redirecting or refocusing an underling. "Right. Well, keep a better hold on your tools. We're already running low on replacements, especially of the gravivariable variety."

"Sure thing, boss. Won't happen again."

Drilling work resumed minutes later, as did the miners' conversations about various topics. Owen did his best to work through the agony in his head. He focused on just getting through his shift. Then he could slam back some pills and sleep the whole thing off. Yet the more time that passed the harder it was for him to focus on anything but the pain. He had to actively fight to stay conscious, nearly missing the chime in his helmet that signaled it was finally time to return to the *Sequana*. The thought of sleep and blissful painkillers sustained him as his suit navigated him back to the sub.

Two pings resonated throughout the water to signal that the defensive drones had been activated once more. The first ripple of sound caused Owen to vomit into his helmet as his vision went pure white. The second threatened to knock him out completely as his chest tightened and a high-pitched whine filled his ears. Fighting through all of this to key up an SOS signal took all of Owen's remaining strength before he succumbed to the sheer torment that was his cranium.

The next thing Owen knew, he awoke to the sound of steady beeping. A quick glance around revealed that he was in one of the *Sequana*'s sickbays. Multiple lines connected to various monitoring equipment that sat next to his bed, and an IV fed a clear fluid into his arm. He didn't have to wait all that long before a nurse noticed he was awake and went to fetch a doctor.

Soon he had three people at his bedside. The first was Isaac, his expression cemented into a half-scowl. The second was the nurse clad in a hospital-white uniform that was perhaps one size too small for him based on how evident his musculature was. The third was a female doctor with an open blue coat, rimmed spectacles, and shoulder-length hair in a bob cut.

"I'm Doctor Minerva. How are you feeling, Mr. Jones?" the doctor asked kindly.

"Like shit," he answered truthfully. "What happened?"

"We were hoping you could tell us that," she replied as she glanced at Isaac. "Far as we were able to discern, you suddenly had an episode on your return to the sub. Yet none of the tests we ran on you could tell us what triggered it or what you experienced."

Despite where he was and what had happened, Owen still felt that he had to only give a half-truth in reply, "A migraine snuck up on me something fierce. Never had one that bad before."

The nurse handed over a tablet to Minerva, who scrolled through it with her index finger. "We did notice your electrolytes were low, and that there was some unusual brain activity when we first brought you in. But after applying a fluid drip your vitals stabilized."

"Then nothing to worry about, right?" Owen asked, uncertain. "I just have to drink more water and stop staying up so late."

After another glance at Isaac, Minerva replied, "Your shift supervisor alerted us to the fact you experienced a major hallucination recently. Normally, that wouldn't be an issue so long as you were handling the psychological fallout. However, I'm concerned that these two events are related. The pressure, both literal and metaphorical, could be causing mental strain that produces both illusions and migraines. Therefore…"

Owen could see where the conversation was headed and did his best to cut her off, "You can't pull me off duty completely! This life is all I know! I can't rotate topside!"

Minerva did her best to soothe him with her words, "I don't think we need to go to that extreme quite yet. I think a full week off would do you some good. Your supervisor here agrees."

Isaac nodded, sternly adding, "Get your head back in the game and come back when you're ready. Do what the doc says."

Helpless, Owen deflated and did his best to put on a brave face. "Fine," he replied.

"Good. Now when I say a week off I mean a week off," Minerva informed him. "No heavy drinking and no trips to the VR suites. Nothing but rest and relaxation. Then I want you back here for a full physical before I clear you to return to work."

"Fine," he repeated as neutrally as he could muster.

Reading the room, Dr. Minerva inclined her head towards her fellow clinicians. As they departed, she added, "We'll swing by in a bit to unhook you and send you back to your quarters. Until then, enjoy the idle time."

Easy for you to say, Owen mentally grumbled back at her. *You're not the one who's going to start at square one in terms of trust and reliability.*

CHAPTER 6
Valentina - Light Lift

The Midnight Hearts' training regimen turned out to be just the right amount of challenging for Valentina. The first day were tests, both physical and mental, to gauge her pre-existing competency. The mental exams she passed without issue. She wasn't a gym bunny or particularly muscular to begin with, but Europa's reduced gravity made physical activity much easier. Despite that, she wouldn't be performing feats of strength either. She had just enough stamina and power to handle the average day out on the ice.

The real stumbling block for her was the lack of knowledge about mining and survival. She knew the basics, sure, yet the tests made it abundantly clear that she was woefully lacking. This meant her instruction was focused upon drilling into her the axioms and methods by which she could both mine safely and extend her survival window should something go wrong. Things like how to use a handheld vibrodrill to start a fire, how to signal in an emergency, and how to handle restroom trips without your nethers freezing. Valentina retained most of the information, though only actual experience on the job would reveal whether any of it had truly stuck.

That's where the VR pods came in. In them Valentina was able to learn how to use different types of vehicles and machinery that were common on work sites. She was tested on different survival scenarios ranging from ice storms to xenos attacks. The latter took her by surprise. The holovids about Europa highlighted that life here was a constant struggle against hostile wildlife, but not to the degree that the lectures and simulations were drilling into her. The local fauna was not just limited to the ocean deep beneath the ice. The ones roaming the surface weren't as hostile, yet still enough of a concern that a third of Valentina's training was spent on what to do in case of an incursion. The recommendations all boiled down to finding a good hiding spot and/or a weapon and hoping help came before any xenos backup arrived. Such a grim course of action served as an effective scare tactic for Valentina, to the point that she had nightmares of gnashing teeth and sharp claws keeping her from proper rest.

Fourteen Europan days passed, though to Valentina it felt more like local months. Regardless of the length of a Europan day, she had little time to get to know her fellow pupils, much less personalize her gear by the time she was boarding a transport to Mining Site 8E. The vehicle was a bus that had large, rotating screws on either side instead of a set of wheels, allowing it to handle most any terrain in exchange for slower speed. The bus would take two days to reach their destination. That meant Valentina and her new co-workers had time to chat.

"...and that's how I got here," finished a brawny man who appeared to be in his late teens. He'd asked everyone to call him "Mouse" for some reason. "Quite the story, eh?"

One of the women besides Valentina, Min Jae-Hwa, wasn't buying Mouse's story. Valentina had observed during training that Min was skeptical of everything, her eyes always narrowing while her arms crossed over her chest, and now that same doubtful inquiry was directed at Mouse. "You mean to imply that you rode a comet halfway here?" she asked incredulously. "And that these 'pirates' you were rescued by lauded you with praise and riches?"

"Yep, that about sums it up!" replied Mouse jovially.

Min rolled her eyes and looked at Valentina. "What about you, Sarah? How'd you end up in the ass end of the solar system?"

She kept her cover story brief, "Work dried up back home, and my family was determined to go 'down with the ship' for some reason or another. It was pretty much either come out here and maybe strike it rich or definitely end up on the streets. I don't know how my family's doing. Didn't bother to check during the trip or when I arrived."

Mouse fidgeted from side to side as he commented, "Eh, they sound like bad eggs anyways! You can always find or form a new family to trust and rely on! And I'm sure we'll all end up buried in our weight in credits!"

A scoff from another man, Hunzuu, met that notion, "More likely we'll end up frozen to death or eaten by rhadas. This is not a good place to be. We are all here because we have nowhere else to go. You would do well to remember that before letting yourself be blinded by the illusion of riches."

"Ahhhh, lighten up, Zuu!" Mouse said as he lightly tapped the darker man's sculpted shoulder with a fist. "You're way too doom and gloom. You gotta remain optimistic! See things as opportunities rather than punishments!"

Valentina jumped in before Hunzuu could retort, "You're one of the few people I've met during training that calls the xenos 'rhadas.' Are you from here, Hunzuu?"

Hunzuu turned to Valentina and dipped his head slowly. "My family has been on Europa for four generations, ever since the first explorers stepped out onto the Carnus Expanse."

"Then why are you with such a backwater mining company?" asked Min doubtingly. "If your family has been here for so long then surely it's well-off enough to land you a cushy life near the Light Lift."

A frown only a step above a scowl met her observation as Hunzuu replied, "You would do well not to call your employer 'backwater.' It is a term off-worlders ignorantly use when talking about Europa and her people. We are just as civilized and advanced as the rest of the solar system."

Min winced under his gaze and quickly apologized, "Alright, I get it. But what about your family then?"

Hunzuu's face relaxed as he continued, "My family does own a few spires near the Light Lift. However, it is tradition that every member of the family experiences what it is like to work both on the Carnus Expanse and within the Sea of Sarpedon before moving onto administrative work near the Lift. I am three years into that journey."

"One cannot be a good supervisor unless they've also worked the same 'lesser' job," Valentina summarized. "Which is why most supervisors and management in general are full of incompetent buffoons."

"Exactly, Sarah," Hunzuu smiled back at her as everyone else nodded along. "I may have misjudged you, for which I apologize. I had thought you were the type of person that relies on status and authority rather than actual skills. Yet only someone who has experienced how empty the former is could make a remark like you just did."

"I think I'm guilty of that too," interjected Mouse. "During training I thought you were just a pretty girl trying way too hard, that you would wash out in a week. Yet here you are, Sarah!"

"You might want to think a little more before attempting flattery, Mouse," sighed Valentina. "Because if that's the best you have to offer then I'm afraid you're going to be perpetually single."

Mouse put a hand over his chest and acted being shot over and over while everyone else laughed at his expense. "You wound me, Sarah! I'll have you know I've been with many fine ladies in my years!"

Before Min could even dispute that notion, Hunzuu's laughter rose over the others. All turned to look at him as he finished chuckling, "Moments of levity such as this are key! This moon is hell made manifest. One wrong move and your life could end. Surviving such a place requires keen wit, luck, and bonds with others. Even Ice Hunters rely on their connections when hunting their prey. That we are already bickering like family is a good sign."

"Even a family has a power structure," Min commented while looking at Valentina. "We'll need to determine who gets to make the big decisions. Personally, my vote's with Sarah here."

A pregnant pause passed in which now everyone present was looking at Valentina. She had no clue why they were so fixated on her, but she intended to find out. "Why me? Surely Hunzuu here, coming from a house that's survived on Europa for nearly a century, is a better choice!"

"Maybe, but he's an uptight bastard!" joked Mouse as he clapped Hunzuu on the back. "I'd much prefer to take direction from a gal like you who is practically oozing natural charisma."

Valentina rolled her eyes back at him. "You can't even take my advice about flirting."

"Nah, I heard you! I just chose to ignore it!"

As those present laughed once more, Valentina used the time to think. She wasn't adept at building a loyal retinue, as evidenced by her lack of one back on Earth. She attributed that primarily to the pressure that Wesler applied with how he hovered around her. Without that bastard here to stunt her growth, Valentina could use this fresh slate to build a solid foundation.

Valentina cleared her throat to get everyone's attention, then offered, "Well, just don't go hero-worshiping me or nonsense like that. I'm the same as any of you out on the ice. Remember what they said in training: 'You can only trust yourself when the chips are down.'"

Most nodded along, though Mouse continued to be the ball of energy he'd been so far, "Pretty *and* humble! You remind me of my older sister!"

"I thought you said you only had two younger brothers," Min pointed out with a sigh. "Which is it?"

As everyone returned to poking holes in Mouse's stories as well as telling their own, Valentina did her best to remain attentive. However, the multitude of names and details were quickly lost on her. She was reminded of the grand balls and parties her family hosted, where she was introduced to so many different people with so many minute details that it quickly became a blur. Her defensive mechanism was to become a wallflower: to be a pretty face whose lack of knowledge or awareness was overlooked thanks to her appearance. Flowers didn't make friends, let alone connections. But here she had to try and break that habit. These could be the people she was stuck with for the rest of her time on Europa.

Valentina remembered little about the fifteen people she was with by the time they reached their destination despite her best efforts. A name, a face, and a single detail about each she could use in conversation. Annoyingly her brain committed more resources to memorize some of Mouse's tall tales. He struck her as the type of person people should look to for advice and leadership. Sure, he talked a big game that largely relied on fanciful storytelling, but he had something to say for almost every occasion. The type of individual who made friends easily and could cheer up anyone. Whereas she felt all she had going for her was her looks at times. She didn't get to dwell on this subject matter for long before the Midnight Hearts Mining Site came into view.

Their transport brought them to the base of Mansrath Highland, a mountain chain of frosted peaks glinting in the sunlight. In a cavernous opening in the mountainside was an encampment surrounded by a high, metal fence. Large conveyor belts brought the raw Gadolinium from deep within the mine, followed by several logistical vehicles inspecting, cataloging, and bundling containers of the ore. These were then picked up by transports beginning on their trek back to the Light Lift. Due to the distance and curvature of the moon, the space elevator had disappeared from the horizon. The only prominent objects there now were these mountains and Jupiter. The Highland provided definition between where the surface ended and the sky began, while Jupiter filled a quarter of the heavens above.

"We're here," called the transport driver as he drove the vehicle up to an airlock on one of the taller buildings of the encampment. "They're expecting you inside. I'd tell ya to enjoy your stay, but I think we all know that would be the n-ice thing to say."

"Right, time to leave!" Valentine yelled as half the occupants groaned at the driver's pun. "Let's go before were subjected to further torture."

"Should we leave Mouse then?" wondered Min as everyone grabbed their bags.

"Hey! I'm not torturing anyone!" he retorted in mock offense. "Okay maybe I did once to this guy on Mars, but..."

"Mouse?" Valentina said plainly.

"Yes?"

"Shut up."

Mouse snapped a salute without pause, "You got it, Boss Sarah!"

CHAPTER 7

Owen - E.S.V. Sequana, Alagonian Depths

Owen was losing his mind. Only three Europan days into his mandated break and he'd already run out of things to do. His colleagues and the other workers on the *Sequana* might be content to do nothing but surf the intranet all day, but not him. Owen felt he'd seen everything worth seeing on the intranet, both visual and audio. New content was scarce. Updates were limited to the rare instances where the *Sequana* journeyed back to the Light Lift for yearly maintenance. That meant most of the intranet's content was generated by the crew, and none of them were able to capture Owen's interest for long.

Owen had done the math: In Earth time he'd been off work for ten and a half days. Another fourteen would pass before he was given a chance to go back to work. Without work to tire him out or provide structure, combined with the inability to go drinking or visit the VR suites, he was going mad. Even as a child he'd had some tasks assigned to him so he contributed to the rest of the ship and its crew. There were no "free rides" on Europa, after all, even for children. But Doctor Minerva had been thorough. To the point that Owen was turned down every time he asked others aboard if he could help or otherwise be assigned some work. He was truly nothing more than dead weight.

Further weighing upon Owen's mind was the feeling that he was being watched. Not by anyone in particular, though. An omnipresent pressure similar to the kind one experienced when working at a terminal while someone watched over their shoulder weighed upon his clavicle and psyche. Sometimes he'd catch sight of something flickering at the edge of his vision, only to find nothing when he whipped around to look. This imposed sentence of rest and relaxation was exacerbating his symptoms. Or, rather, the lack of meaningful distraction meant Owen couldn't simply ignore these frustrating thoughts. Only one loophole to Doctor Minerva's rules existed that could provide some measure of comfort: Red Deck, specifically the Pleasure Halls.

Owen had never been to the Pleasure Halls of *Sequana*'s Red Deck, though not for lack of funds or a drive to experience such things. He was in his final teenage year, after all. He had the drive in spades. Yet he had been so committed to his work and his VR hobbies that he never had time for it. He also wasn't secure in his sexuality. Exploring it just hadn't been a priority in his life. But now, faced with too much free time and specters haunting him, he eventually worked up the courage to go.

Like most Europan Red Decks, the *Sequana*'s Red Deck was quite literally a part of the ship that had bright red corridors that were wider than normal, in addition to dimmer lighting. The entire deck was filled with loud music, catcalls, and people having a good time. This was thanks largely to the various bars and strip clubs opened up into this space. Past them were individual parlors where the independent adult entertainers worked.

Normal natives of Earth would have looked down upon the salacious activities that took place there. But to anyone who served on a ship, no matter what ocean, sky, or space it traveled in, this was accepted practice. After all, there was a reason the saying of "100 people go down and 50 couples come back up" was common among submariners. Humans naturally sought out such delights and physical connection, especially with the amount of stress that inhabitants of the Sea of Sarpedon experienced day to day.

Today's Red Deck was boisterous as usual. Owen walked by bars blasting Earth rock music and past clubs with entrances obscured by the bright neon lights surrounding them. The crowd wasn't that difficult to navigate, though Owen was thankful to have some elbow room when the throng began to thin out towards the parlors. Here instead of fancy signs, promises of liquor, and the usual advertisement were actual people. Men, women, and everything in between strutted and stretched their stuff in an attempt to attract customers to their parlors. In a way, Owen and the other few patrons still around were window shopping.

That same sense of being watched now had a tangible form for Owen. He felt like he was being judged just for coming to the Pleasure Halls. Similar to how people sometimes viewed sex workers as nothing but meat, he imagined himself as nothing more than a walking wallet. Every once and a while he caught the eye of an escort trying to entice him in, only for their gaze to turn cold when he kept moving. Some even turned their nose up at him with a sneer. Such a reaction was disheartening for Owen, to say the least. He was about to give up and return to his meager quarters when he focused on someone towards the stern end of Red Deck.

They were slim, fit, and curved in all the right places. Long silver hair with blood-red streaks spilled down in waves across their shoulders and form-fitting azure dress. What attracted Owen to them was their smile: a genuine one that radiated the kind of joy and safety that Owen needed.

"Uh, hi," Owen nervously stated as he moved closer to them. "I'm… I'm here for…"

The individual continued to grin as they replied sweetly, "Take your time, hun. Whatever you need, I can help. I'm Skye."

"Right. I'm uh… Owen. And, well, I have no idea how any of this works. I've never been to this part of Red Deck."

"There's a first time for everything, hun, not to worry. You're the one in control here. Though perhaps you would like to discuss it inside?"

Skye motioned to the parlor door. Owen gulped, nodded, and went inside. The interior was twice the size of his quarters. A circular bed took up most of the space, covered in luxurious furs and rich silks. The lighting was provided by dim LEDs disguised as candles scattered about the place. The scent of what Owen had been told in his youth was a rose wafted through the air.

Skye led him to the edge of the bed to sit, then sat next to him. A moment of silence passed before Owen found his tongue again. His confidence wavered. He managed to babble, "Can we just… talk? I know I could have just gone to the bar or an intranet chat room but…"

In the torturous time it took Skye to respond, Owen almost wished a Leviathan would eat him. That notion was dispelled when Skye gave him a soft side hug and said, "I'd be happy to talk. Truth be told, there's a reason I'm so far back on Red Deck. Not many people seek out my kind of services."

"That's a shame. You seem, uh… nice," Owen responded as he enjoyed the hug.

Skye pulled back, giggling, "Well thank you! But this isn't about me. What's on your mind, hun? No judgment here. We can talk about whatever it is you want."

It took some time before Owen slowly replied, "I'm worried I'm going to have to rotate topside."

"Why's that?"

"I've… I've been seeing things. Leviathans and rhadas in general sneaking up on me. I know they're not the real thing, but I'm worried I'm cracking. Especially after I found that strange object and started to feel pain whenever a drone halfway across the mining site launched a sonic attack on probing rhadas. Now I can't shake the feeling that someone or something is watching me."

"That seems awful. I'm sorry you're having to go through something like that. If I'm being honest, I've definitely had clients that have expressed similar things when the stress starts to get to them. But never something like the pain you just mentioned. Have you seen a doctor about it?"

Owen sighed deeply, "That's why I'm here now. I'm on 'Medical Leave' for a week. No real friends to hang out with, no booze, no VR suites, just rest and relaxation as per doctor's orders. But being cooped up in my room wasn't helping anything. I needed to get out."

"I see. I'm glad you came here then. Would leaving the ocean really be all that bad?" Skye asked tenderly.

"Yes," Owen immediately replied. Then he walked it back somewhat by explaining, "Er, I think it wouldn't be fun. I grew up down here. Came with my dad when I was nine. And even when he… left… I ended up staying in the ocean. It's the only kind of life I really know."

"Hmm. If you don't mind sharing, what happened to him? Your father, I mean. No pressure though. Share what feels comfortable."

His eyes closed as he recalled the day in question. "It was halfway through beta shift when two Leviathans and a swarm of rhadas ambushed the *E.S.V. Sirena* and its mining site. Dad was out on the eastern fringe. I was aboard the *Sirena* hiding in our room. Somehow, the *Sirena* managed to escape. When the alarms, shouting, and explosions stopped, I kept waiting for him to return. But he never did. Instead, one of his friends on gamma shift came and told me that Dad had been eaten in the first assault wave. Not killed, not smashed, not any of those things. *Eaten.* That's always stayed with me. It likely will never truly go away."

A reassuring hand from Skye came to rest on his lap. "Can I let you in on a little secret, Owen? Everyone down here didn't just decide to hate the rhadas on a whim. Everyone hates them for real reasons like the one you just shared. But that's also the point - Everyone is broken in some way. Some are just better at hiding it."

He pulled away, making to stand. "You're right. I should just suck it up and learn to hide my feelings. If everyone else is able to do it then I'll have to as well."

"That's not what I meant at all, hun," Skye said as they stopped him from rising and gently tugged him back to his seat. "We live in an environment where everything can be turned upside-down in mere moments. It would be crazy to *not* be a little insane. You aren't alone in your struggles. Yet that doesn't trivialize or otherwise dismiss them. What you're going through sounds wretched. But you don't have to deal with it entirely on your own. Does that make sense to you?"

Owen considered that notion for a time. Then he answered, "I suppose. I've just been on my own for nine years. Reaching out for help is hard for me."

"You should only do it if you're ready. That said, there are no magic words or pills that can help you. It may sound harsh, but only *you* can ultimately choose to make a change for the better. Other people can simply help you find your way back onto your feet. Sometimes talking things out with a good listener can help you realize what you need to do."

"But what am I supposed to do about the hallucinations? What if there's something really wrong with me?"

Skye winked at him. "Somehow, I don't think there is. At least, not in the way you're worrying about. I think your subconscious is trying to tell you something."

Owen turned to study them closely. "Like, what? That I need to face the past and get over it? That holding onto pain and being a loner is killing me? That fear is making me weak?"

"No, but those are all good insights," Skye smiled and pointed a finger at him. "I suggest you think further on each. As well as something I'm sure you've heard asked rhetorically before: Do you know what a blind man needs with an aquarium?"

"I can't say I do," Owen answered truthfully. "But I have seen that asked a few times on the intranet. I thought it was just a meme meant to draw people into an argument or pointless debate."

Skye continued to grin as they stood and brought Owen with them. "Give it some thought all the same. It might be more relevant to your situation than you think.

Owen turned to Skye with eyes full of inner turmoil. "Right… I'm going to need some time. And a walk. How much do I, uh, owe you?"

Skye placed strong, yet delicate, fingers around his and escorted him towards the door still wearing that smile. "Talking's free, hun. Though if you really want to pay me, bring back a bottle of whiskey."

Owen wasn't about to argue with that. "Deal."

His head tilted in a departing bow, then he stepped out of the parlor, and started walking. Luckily for him, the *Sequana* was plenty big enough for the type of introspective walk he needed to go on.

CHAPTER 8
Thatch - Dark Lift

The *E.F.S.V. Wolffish* finally came to a stop as it docked with the cylindrical support structure leading up out of the ocean and towards the Dark Lift. Power lines, walkways, and other umbilicals moved to meet the ship from the jutting spire that were a part of a larger snowflake design. Compared to the Light Lift, the immediate area wasn't nearly as busy and full of movement. Freight haulers and cargo transfer vehicles still moved about the ocean, just not the frantic frenzy and carefully calculated chaos that was found on the opposite side of Europa. Here, things were slower, more deliberate. Pirates, mercenaries, and other ne'er do wells that called to port here lived by the unspoken rule that you never messed with the logistics. A rule that had been enforced by the current Grand Admiral in charge of the Dark Lift and his fleet for over fifty years. Practically one and a half lifetimes for the average Europan.

"I always love how different the air tastes here," said Volodina as she, Yukawa, and Thatch cycled through one of the *Wolffish*'s airlocks into one of the station's support lines.

All three were wearing their finest furs fashioned in the colors of the Dread Lurkers: raven-black, snow-white, and hunter-green. Their logo, a sinewy serpent coiled in and around a toxic-hued heart, was prominent on their shoulders, hats, and chests. Actual swords were sheathed on Yukawa's and Volodina's belts, whereas Thatch's sported a cruel, thorned whip. The display of power and wealth was how people moving about the station knew who not to mess with and who to clear out for if ever they came in sight. But even then, that didn't stop some brave souls from trying something anyway.

"It's just your imagination," Yukawa commented as the three walked. "I can't smell anything worth noting."

"Ah, but that's where you're wrong!" retorted Volodina as Thatch looked on. "Even down here you can still get a whiff of those delectable spices they use in cooking and the fragrances of the hookah bars. Maybe your nose is just broken."

"Could be. I did get punched rather hard when I was a child. Practically shattered my nose. It's a miracle it reformed."

"I suppose that explains why you're so ugly then. I--," Volodina stopped as Thatch shot her a look. "Sorry, Admiral. Where are we headed?"

"We have a meeting with Grand Admiral Triton in his palace, followed by catching up with Captain O'Dea at the Rusty Bucket," Thatch explained. "The Grand Admiral visit shouldn't take long. Just the standard lip service and tithe promise."

"Good. That place is a death trap," Yukawa shuddered. "It's different every time we have to go there, and there's always the stench of death around it."

"Oh, so you can smell death but not the curry in the air?" Volodina sneered.

"Entirely different matters. But let us table that discussion for later. Our Admiral looks ready to whip us both into shape."

Thatch didn't really intend for such a thing. All she'd done was move her hand to rest on the top of her whip. That was all it took for her two crewmates to remember their place. There was a certain level of authority that she naturally exuded. One that people gravitated towards and respected. And she owned every bit of it. It had been so long since she actually had to whip someone that she barely remembered the instigating incident.

The trio reached the solid ground of the dock and found their way towards one of the many lifts at the center of the crystalline-inspired architecture. Dock workers bowed their heads as they passed by, as did several lesser-ranking Captains that stopped their arguing once they saw Thatch. The only individual who didn't bow was the man Triton had sent to meet them at the lifts. As fine as his clothes were, the azure icosahedron with a dual Leviathans flanking it was what truly projected the weight and level of his social status above that of Thatch.

"Admiral Thatch," the man said as the trio arrived at the central ring of the station. "My name is Wo. I trust your journey here was fruitful and without cause for concern?"

As was expected of her, Thatch reached into her sleeve and produced a physical twenty-sided die in the same color and markings as Triton's logo on Wo's clothing. She showed it to Wo, specifically showing the number 17. It was part of a semi-secret code among all Admirals that paid tribute to Grand Admiral Triton. A 17 meant they only required refueling and resupplying, and that the goods in their cargo hold should cover the costs. Triton was efficient when it came to logistics like this. He had worked out the perfect way to control and coordinate all the little moving parts of the controlled chaos that was the Dark Lift, both in the Sea of Sarpedon and on the surface above.

"Very good then," Wo continued as Thatch slipped the die away without saying a word. "Grand Admiral Triton is expecting you. I will see you to him directly."

He turned without even waiting for acknowledgement and proceeded into one of the waiting lifts. Volodina started to comment on Wo's lack of confirmation but withered when Thatch looked at her. The three joined Wo in the lift and began their journey upwards to the surface. The smooth ride of the elevator as it passed through the twenty-kilometer-thick ice shell that separated the Sea of Sarpedon below and the Carnus Expanse above happened in silence. Neither Thatch, her subordinates, or Wo broke the silence of the perpetual waiting room without any entertainment or distractions. Thatch herself dealt with the pressure just fine, as did Yukawa. Volodina's nervous fidgeting earned her several biting glances from Owen but did not attract either Thatch's or Wo's attention. Though neither could miss the huge sigh of relief Volodina let out when the doors opened.

On the other side of the threshold was the Grand Admiral's palace. As the tallest skyscraper on the dark side of Europa, the view across the Carnus Expanse out of the windows was unmatched. The runner-up building was nearly half the size and half as likely to cause nausea when looking to its top. Despite the palace being cloaked in perpetual darkness, enough lights projected upon it for Thatch to pick out the azure marbling in the dark stonework. Stone leviathans loomed like classical Earth gargoyles at the roof corners. Wo led them across the courtyard to ornate double doors that could withstand a direct blast. The doors opened as he approached, light spilling out as Thatch and her crew entered.

The interior was similarly a peacock display, though not because of the expensive art, rare construction materials, or even the multiple fountains. Instead, it was the ambient temperature: a balmy 12°C. To afford such heating even in a mostly-empty lobby like this was by far one of the largest projections of power on Europa. Thatch and her crew longed for the cooler temperatures found beneath the ice thanks to the multitude of layers they had on.

Wo led them through the lobby to another set of elevators. This time, the ride only took minutes before they arrived at the Grand Admiral's penthouse and another set of blast doors. Thatch knew what to expect having been here before, as did Yukawa, but Volodina let out confused noises when the doors opened. Volodina was expecting an even finer collection of material goods than in the lobby. Yet the room was the modest interior of a Shinto-style Haiden, or hall of worship. The floor was covered by a charcoal-colored tatami mat, with walls that matched the marbling of the building's exterior. Two umber vases in the far corners bearing the Grand Admiral's sigil were the only other objects in the room.

The Grand Admiral was seated upon a cushion with his legs crossed in meditation. His loose robes billowed at the sleeves and left his chest bare for the onlookers to see how heavily scarred his body was. His face was weathered, an unyielding pillar shaped by the fierce winds of Europa and multiple attempts on his life. One eye was covered by a patch, while the other opened as Wo and the trio stepped off the lift.

"I have brought your guests, Grand Admiral," Wo said, genuflecting before Triton. "May I present--"

"I know who they are," Triton said, his voice like a never-ending avalanche. "Leave us."

Wo bowed deeply before skittering off through a side door previously indistinguishable from the surrounding wall. That left Thatch, Yukawa, and Volodina alone with Triton. The Yukawa and Volodina were sweating at this point, and not just because of the higher-than-normal temperature. This man could upend their entire lives and those of their fellow crew with the same effort it took to breathe. Yukawa and Volodina flinched when Thatch greeted Triton in such a familiar tone:

"I see you've redecorated since the last time. Wasn't there an actual gemstone and mirror in here before?"

Triton let out a low, rumbling chuckle, "After the last two assassination attempts I had them moved back into the honden. No sense in keeping them on display where they'll get damaged."

"Wait here," Thatch said to her underlings before moving forward and sitting before Triton in a mirrored manner. Then to the Grand Admiral, she offered, "I'm happy to report I can offer a 2% increase in the tithe this month. Hunting has been good all around."

"Hmm. I see. Tell me, Thatch, are you aiming for my head?"

As Volodina and Yukawa looked at one another and blanched, Thatch answered without missing a beat, "Maybe one day, old man, but not today. I just wanted to give you a little extra in appreciation for handling that premium shipment of black ice from one of my captains."

Triton rose, and Thatch followed. The two stared at one another for so long that the tension was thicker than Europa's ice, a custom among denizens of the dark side to gauge one's respect and gumption. Then they both smiled and shook hands. Afterwards, Triton asked, "Before you go, have you given more thought to that question I asked you years ago?"

Thatch chuckled, "The whole blind man and the aquarium one? If so, my answer hasn't changed. The only purpose such an aquarium serves is a place the blind man can be guaranteed to catch a fish in."

Triton sighed, shook his head, then turned away without a further word. Recognizing that as a sign of dismissal, Thatch returned to her underlings as Triton returned to his seat. It was only once the lift doors had closed that both Yukawa and Volodina began questioning what had just happened.

"Admiral, what the hell is your relationship to the Grand Admiral?" asked Yukawa in wonder. "No offense meant, Ma'am."

"None taken, first mate. I was once a part of his crew, way back when he roamed the ocean instead of administrating from the surface," explained Thatch. "I learned a lot from him thanks to being his 'favorite redshirt.'"

"As in he put you in the most dangerous of situations?" inquired Volodina in awe. "Edge of mining operations, leading boarding parties, and all that?"

"Indeed. Anyone else probably would have kicked the bucket a few years in. Or transferred off. But I stuck with it. I learned later that was Triton's way of tempering me through fire. It's thanks to him why I even have the *Wolffish* now."

"I never knew…" Yukawa mused. "I'm guessing you don't want the rest of the crew to know?"

He furtively glanced at the stunned Volodina. Thatch caught it and nodded ever so slightly at him. She didn't mind if this secret reached the public, as every other Admiral already knew. Part of the reason she'd brought Volodina today was to test her loyalty and ability to keep a secret. Thatch was nothing if not pragmatic.

"I'd prefer it if you kept a lid on this, yes. Don't dwell on this long. We still have O'Dea to meet."

After another long transit back down into the depths of Europa, Thatch and her crew made for the glorified hole-in-the-wall bar that was the Rusty Bucket. It had two things going for it: cheap booze and a killer sound system. Even halfway around the promenade Thatch could still hear the guitar riffs belting out from the bar. That was one of the reasons she'd chosen this location to meet O'Dea. Conversations tended to get lost in all the noise, which meant there was little worry of eavesdroppers.

The main reason, though, was that every trip she'd ever taken to the Rusty Bucket had ended in a fun little adventure. Last time a long night of drinking with strangers led her to a rich Black Ice deposit. What it held for her today was a mystery.

The bar's grungy interior matched the literal rusted bucket hanging above the door outside. The loud, wailing music wafting from the interior made one lose their thoughts, which was sort of the point. If you weren't thinking you were drinking and vice versa. A healthy number of patrons were scattered about the place between bar stools, booths, and around the few holo-game tables that somehow never got damaged. O'Dea was saving Thatch a curved booth towards the rear of the place.

"Took you long enough!" he shouted and stood as Thatch walked up to him. "I was beginning to think the Grand Admiral actually called you on your bullshit for once!"

Thatch met his offered hand before motioning for Yukawa and Volodina to take the seats on the left side of the booth. Then she herself slipped into the middle-right with O'Dea right behind her.

"Nah, the elevators were just stupidly slow as per usual," Thatch replied jovially. "I keep telling the Grand Admiral he needs to increase their speed but he never listens."

After a robo-server took their orders and floated back to the bar, O'Dea lowered his voice to ask, "So, why are we meeting here instead of on-ship?"

"Simple, Captain. We're keeping up appearances," explained Thatch in a similar manner. "If I'm not seen being social and doing business, then people will start to forget I exist. And when you don't exist to someone it's very easy for them to knock you off without a second thought."

The double implication was not lost on O'Dea or Yukawa, though it did go over Volodina's head. "Aye, I can understand that, Admiral," O'Dea replied. "So, what sort of business is on the table?"

"That Black Ice you harvested and brought in, actually. I've heard of several reports and rumors that imply it's some of the purest strains ever to grace the Dark Lift."

O'Dea regarded her carefully. "You thinking of going back there? Sure, it was a great payout, but It's not worth the risk."

Thatch flashed him a sly smirk as she said, "I simply want to know how you came across it in the first place. Was it luck, or did someone give you a juicy tip?"

"Little of both, actually. An old geezer here on the station gave me the coordinates when I gave him some credits. I didn't think much of them until I was already in the general area on patrol."

"Then it occurs to me that we should pay this 'old geezer' a visit to see if he has any more such coordinates secreted away."

Yukawa interrupted and pointed, "You might want to wait on that, Admiral."

She followed his finger to see that three burly men in gaudy, golden furs had entered the bar and were beelining for her booth. She took a swig of her drink just so she finished by the time they reached her.

"And what can I do for you fine gentlemen?" Thatch asked in a neutral manner. "Did you get lost on the way to the bathroom? It's just through that door there. Though I wouldn't bother. You're going to smell like shit no matter what you do."

The man in charge of the golden boys slammed his hands down on her table as he declared, "You and I are going to duel, witch! For the honor of the Glimmering Guppies."

Volodina burst out laughing as the rest of the table grinned. Thatch was quick to retort, "I wasn't aware that such small fry were even allowed onto the station. Why should I even grace you with the time of day?"

Her words riled up the man further. He roared back, ripping the table free of the floor and flinging it out into the bar. An impressive display of strength but not a concerning one. O'Dea, Yukawa, and Volodina all looked to Thatch to see how she reacted. With a sigh, she rose, plucked up her whip, and flicked it so it snapped against the ground right before the bruiser. "I hadn't quite finished my drink yet, whelp. Now are you going to get me a new one or do I have to teach you a further lesson?"

The right hook aimed at her face was the only answer she required. She moved like water, flowing around the punch while swirling her whip out to give it momentum. Her knee drove right into the man's stomach, causing him to reel backwards into the waiting whip end. The vicious slap was enough to send him spiraling to the ground in pain. His fellows weren't far behind. Thatch dispatched them with only two further whip cracks before sitting back down in her original seat.

"Put the table and any damages on my tab!" she yelled at the barkeep. Then to the defeated buffoons, she added, "I'll give you some kudos for trying the 'stand up to the biggest person in the place' tactic, but that only works if you actually have the brawns AND the brains to back it up. All you've done is made a laughing stock of yourselves and your Gloaming Gulps or whatever it is you are. Now run along with your tail between your legs. Unless you would prefer another lesson?"

They declined her generous offer. By the time they were gone, a new table had been delivered along with fresh drinks. The rest of the bar's patrons whistled at and toasted Thatch at the insistence of O'Dea and Yukawa. Volodina remained frozen in shock. As for Thatch, she relished the attention and enjoyed her drink with less reserve than before.

CHAPTER 9

Valentina - Midnight Hearts Mining Site, Carnus Expanse

Surface mining was simultaneously the hardest and easiest thing Valentina had ever done. The actual act of vibrodrilling out chunks of Gadolinium was physically intense but mentally numbing. Conversely, controlling the cargo lifters and cranes required tremendous mental focus but kept her couped up in a small control booth. She couldn't afford to let her concentration lapse without risk of breaking equipment or injuring other miners. Not unlike how she had to constantly worry about whatever Wesler's newest plan for her was. One slip up borne from lack of focus and she'd end up back in Wesler's clutches. Valentina honestly couldn't decide which form of tasking she preferred. Above it all, though, she finally felt as if she were free. No one looming over her like her parents, no pressure to be the perfect wife-material for a man she loathed. She was making her own way on her own terms. Her fellow workers had started to feel like her new family.

Every night she joined Mouse, Min, Hunzuu, and the others from her shift around the heater in the common area of their dorm hall. They laughed, drank, played games, and generally swapped stories of their lives. And tonight was her turn to do most of the talking.

"Don't keep us waiting, Boss Sarah!" encouraged Mouse. "We wanna hear about our fearless leader!"

Valentina sighed, "We've been over this, Mouse. I'm not your leader. That's Foreman Bentham."

"Nah he's just the guy we listen to to get work done. You're like our spiritual leader. Way more important. Why I remember one time--"

Min cut Mouse off before he could start telling another one of his stories, "What he's trying to say is that everyone wants to know where you come from. Why you came to Europa. That sort of thing."

A look between everyone present confirmed to Valentina that this was the case. She had been deliberately vague up to this point in the hopes it wouldn't attract further attention, but it seemed she'd have to put her cover story to the test once again. With reluctance, she sighed, took in a deep breath, and began:

"I know some of you are from Earth, so parts of this will sound familiar. For those of you that have never been, I'm sure you think of Earth as some beautiful blue jewel and a true utopia. Everyone's happy, has a place to live, gets a good education, and generally can pursue any career or higher learning they wish. Sound familiar so far?"

A few people nodded. Those who had come from Earth, like Min, remained stony-faced as Valentina continued, "That's the truth the media wants you to know. The truth is that Earth has become the home for the elite and their servants. Slaves might be a better word, really. You're either working for a 'nobleborn,' teaching future generations, performing research, or otherwise serving a supporting role. Everyone else is shipped off-world to Luna, Mars, and the outer colonies like Europa."

Valentina paused in hesitation before continuing. She hadn't lied yet about the state of Earth. The feeling of being in a gilded cage contributed to why she found it so easy to leave in the first place. But now her story had to enter into falsehoods to keep her family from finding her.

"I was a dancer for one of the noble families in the Russian Federation. A glorified court jester meant to twirl about for the delight of others. But one of the sons of the family began to covet me in an obsessive manner. He'd have me dance hours on end, then force me to listen to his awful stories about how hard it was to run his family's business. I realized one day that if that kept up, one day he'd go further and truly force himself on me. And as I wasn't nobleborn, I couldn't say no to that."

"Therefore, you escaped," observed Hunzuu as he finished off his bowl of soup. "How did you manage that?"

Valentina lowered her voice and was pleased to see everyone leaning in to listen. "Well, it took a lot of favors and connections. I had to be smuggled out in the dead of night disguised as part of the trash. Not very glamorous, I assure you. From there I had to disguise myself and take circuitous routes until I arrived at the spaceport in Berlin. The first ship out was one to Europa. I suppose I could have waited for something else, but I'd always enjoyed the stories of Ice Hunters that came from here. So it was both out of necessity and following the familiar that I ended up here. The rest you pretty much already know."

Light muttering broke out as those gathered discussed her tale. To her relief, she didn't see, hear, or otherwise notice any signs that anyone was doubting her truthfulness. She'd practiced that story a hundred times during the flight from Earth to Europa. There were elements of truth in it, which probably made her sound all the more sincere. She wasn't out of the woods quite yet, though. She still had to survive the inevitable barrage of questions.

Mouse spoke up first, "So you're from Russia? I guess the stories my cousin used to tell about how pretty the girls were are all true! But what kind of dancing are we talking about? Ballet? Ballroom? Salsa? Anything you could teach us?"

Biting back a comment at his subtle pass at her, Valentina answered, "Ballroom and Belly Dancing, actually. The former's easy to teach, but the latter requires you to have mastery over your gut."

Min was quick to comment, "Good. The thought of Mouse belly dancing is horrific enough to wish death by Leviathan."

"Hey now! I have great control over my gut!" protested Mouse. "I just don't show it off because you'd all be jealous."

"I dunno, Mouse, the thought of you trying to belly dance is pretty hilarious," Valentina snickered. "Definitely court jester material."

"Fine! I'll prove it to you all!"

Mouse stood and wiggled like an earthworm fleeing the dirt after the rain. An absurd display that got everyone laughing. In this moment, Valentina saw Mouse as the kind of person to do whatever he could to make people laugh and feel entertained. Ironically the best kind of court performer. And that was his strength. He may have struggled with the manual labor of mining during the day, but here he was in his element and full of life. Something for her to emulate once she made it into the Sisters of Solace. Although perhaps not Mouse's belly dancing. She was pretty sure she was far more skilled than Mouse's flailing in that department.

Once Mouse finally gave up and sat back down amid laughter, Min spoke up with her own question, "Do you want to be an Ice Hunter then, Sarah?"

Valentina nodded, "That's the plan, yes. I have my eyes on the Sister of Solace. Part of the reason I'm out here is to gain survival skills and to become acclimated to the decreased gravity."

Mouse whistled as Hunzuu pointed out, "The Sisters of Solace are quite exclusive. I mean no disrespect, but how do you see yourself gaining entry into their order?"

Pointing at Mouse, Valentina joked, "I'll bring Mouse in for one of his many, many crimes. I mean, he's been a pirate, a thief like 'Robin Hood,' and pretty much just violated public decency by doing whatever the hell that wiggling was."

The whole room, including Mouse, erupted in chuckles. Valentina fielded a few more questions from the audience, none of which were particularly revealing. Things like her favorite color (sea green), how she kept her hair so silky smooth, and other benign inquiries that didn't test the limits of her story. Once that was over it was time for everyone to retreat back to bed before another long shift the next day.

Or, it would have been if a klaxon didn't begin wailing across the mining site. A signal of three wails followed by two chirps. The noise meant one thing: xenos were coming.

The gathered crowd split. Most went scurrying for the bunker in the basement of the dormitory. Only Valentina, Min, Mouse, Hunzuu, and a handful of others stayed and moved towards the transparent aluminum windows. Spotlights were all directed towards the northern wall where the defensive railguns were spooling up and the spotters were painting targets. Valentina remembered how imposing the guns seemed on her way into the mining site, how she couldn't imagine what warranted such heavy weaponry.

That notion evaporated as the xenos came into the light. They were twisted creatures, hexapods that stole elements from animals back on Earth. A shark-like head with gnashing teeth; a long, serpentine body with claws and spikes that glittered in metallic fashion; and a fur coat that would make a wooly mammoth jealous. There were ten xenos, each the size of one of the cargo lifters Valentina had used earlier in the day and all large enough to loom several heads over an average human's.

"The media feeds don't do them justice," Valentina commented as the muffled discharge of railguns resonated through the mining site. "They're far more terrifying and larger than anything I remember seeing before coming here."

Hunzuu took up the spot to her left at the window and responded impassively, "You would do well to pray to whatever god you believe in that this is not a vanguard for a larger force. The surface may be safer than the ocean, but the rhadas here are just as deadly as the great Leviathans below. The media does not tell of this for fear of scaring off new blood. Nor does the training we received adequately explain the level of danger the rhadas present."

"I can see that," she said as she watched two xenos being struck through the crowns of each of their heads by supersonic tungsten rods. "But it's only at the mining sites that they actively attack people, right? Why is that?"

"Some say the rhadas attack is because the materials we mine resonate with them. That they are connected far more intensely with Europa than any animal on Earth. Others speculate that the mining sites are the loudest and easiest prey out on the ice. The truth is unclear."

Several more railguns spooled up and began launching payloads at the incoming xenos. Valentina couldn't help but picture one of the creatures reaching the defensive wall and smashing through it like paper. Yet, the weapon batteries finally dealt enough damage to force the xenos to retreat. Only three of them had been slain while the other seven limped off leaving trails of dark blue blood on the ice in their wake. Once out of sight, a signal of four rising chirps signaled an all-clear. The mining site resumed operation as if nothing had happened.

"So, we're back to normal, just like that?" sighed Valentina as she turned away from the window. "I know that's what our training said is supposed to happen but I thought it would have... I don't know... taken a lot longer."

"Time is money, after all!" offered Mouse jovially. "Reminds me of the time my second cousin..."

The four of them groaned and dispersed before Mouse could tell another fanciful tale. Yet as Valentina slipped into her bunk and tried to sleep, her thoughts were cluttered with images of the xenos charging the mining defenses relentlessly. The search for dreams took a majority of the night.

CHAPTER 10

Owen - Blue Bison Mining Site, Alagonian Depths

A wave of relief washed over Owen when he was finally able to resume his usual mining duties. Despite being cooped up in his pressure suit, he no longer felt like he was in the cage bearing the name *Sequana*. He'd managed to stay sane by visiting Skye several more times during his forced vacation. Skye was surprisingly wise for someone that called Red Deck home. Owen had a hunch Skye had been a miner at one point, but never asked in an attempt to be polite.

Today's alpha shift started with Owen working with two newbies (Liam and Jasper) who had rotated down into Europa's ocean a few days ago. Their goal was to dislodge a mining drone whose reactor unexpectedly shut down mid-drilling and return it to the *Sequana* for proper repair. The drone was powerless and buried beneath rubble that had fallen across it like a collapsing gingerbread house.

Regardless of what work it might take to get the drone out, Owen was just glad to have a chance to stretch his legs in a meaningful manner. "Alright, on three we all pull. Got it?" he asked Liam and Jasper as the three of them gained handholds on the mining drone. They had cleared what they could of the fallen rock and debris. Now they had to rely on their own strength and leverage to get the drone out.

"Got it," both newbies replied.

Owen counted down. All three men grunted and strained but the mining drone remained firmly lodged in place.

"Damn," grunted Owen as he waved for everyone to stop. "It's really in there. We're going to have to dig more of it out, even if that means we damage the drone in the process. Set your vibrodrills to low resonance and take it slow."

As the three began excavation work, Owen wished he could use another drone or one of the *Sequana*'s articulating arms to wrench this drone out. Either would save hours of work that could have gone towards actual mining. Unfortunately, he and the other two simply lacked the strength on their own to get the drone out, and there wasn't enough spare, working equipment to go around this shift.

To make matters worse, the newbies weren't much for bantering. Owen tried several times to get them talking but they continued to fall into silence. This was a complete reversal from Owen's first mission half a decade ago where his boss at the time threatened to rip out his comms unit if Owen kept blathering on. These newbies were too stiff for his liking. Sure, they were being cautious and feeling out their new situation. That much Owen could empathize with. But to him, you either learned to live in the moment down here in the Sea of Sarpedon or you set yourself up to have your hopes, dreams, loves, and more crushed without warning.

A sonic ping interrupted the slow, methodical unburying. Owen didn't experience any pain this time, though he did pick up on the sound far easier than he recalled doing so in the past. The ping echoed both through his helmet's speakers and through the water around him thanks to his proximity to the edge of the mining site. He also was able to pick out the swirling tentacles and other appendages of the rhadas that had tried to enter into the mining site. Strangely, there was just one. And it had attempted to cross the boundary closest to him. That worried Owen. It was possible that somehow the work in getting this drone out was stirring up the rhadas more than other work across the mining site.

"Let's speed this thing up," Owen ordered. "Better to have a damaged drone than no drone at all."

The trio worked faster. Again, Owen wished for something powerful enough to just rip the damn thing free. Then three more pings and an anti-rhadas torpedo launch rebuffed new arrivals at the perimeter. At this point he didn't care if the drone ended up becoming a hunk of scrap metal. He wanted his task over and done with so he could slink away to the safety of the *Sequana*.

That's when Owen heard a sound he hadn't heard for years. The highest-level alert siren could only mean one thing: a Leviathan was inbound. Blood drained away from his face as swore, tossed his vibrodrill aside, and tried to pull the drone free out of desperation to no avail. "We're going to have to abandon it. Back to the *Sequana,* quickly!"

The newbies didn't need telling twice. Owen was right behind them as they swam for the relative safety that the *Sequana* offered. Every other individual on alpha shift and the few irreplaceable drones they could afford to wait on were beelining for the *Sequana*. Protocol was clear: Drones could be replaced. Workers could not. Ironically, they would be leaving behind more drones that would have to be dug out later. But nothing could be done about it. Leviathans were not something to be trifled with. Even the *Sequana* and her escorts would be hard-pressed to turn back such a beast without collateral damage.

Understandably, Owen experienced several flashbacks to that day nine years ago when his father was killed. How he was forced to hide in a space smaller than his current quarters as alarms and sirens mixed with horrific screeches of metal and rhadas. How the deck pitched and yawed like how roller coasters supposedly worked on Earth. This encouraged him to swim faster, to get as far away from the incoming beast as possible.

Looking over his shoulder Owen saw the defensive drones forming an impromptu wall of lights as they clustered up in the direction of the Leviathan. Then they were smashed, crushed, and tossed aside as the Leviathan's massive, sinewy body slammed through them like a bowling ball through wet paper. A horrendous, bone-chilling roar came from the creature as its full length lit up in bioluminescence. Its body seemed to stretch on forever in the darkness, to the point trying to comprehend the Leviathan's size strained Owen's mind. But what frightened Owen the most were the creatures' triple-pupiled eyes. They were locked straight ahead directly on Owen, or so he imagined.

A gruff, seasoned voice came over the comm network, "This is Captain Harman of the *Sequana*. All hands, prepare for tactical maneuvering. All divers not aboard stop your approach and seek shelter."

Owen's stomach flipped at Captain Harman's words. He, Liam, and Jasper had been too slow and missed their ride to safety.

"Dive to the seabed!" Owen shouted as he dove for the closest outcropping that jutted out from the ocean floor.

He spared no glance or second thought for the newbies. Instead, he continued to watch in awe and horror as the Leviathan continued its advance. The Leviathan was heading straight for that same drone Owen had been working on. Jaws capable of crushing the *Sequana* opened wide and consumed both the drone and the surrounding rock like a vacuum in less time than it took to blink.

"Alright, you got what you came here for," Owen whispered in prayer. "Now just leave. Don't come any closer. Just go away."

To his horror, the Leviathan swung its head around so its eye looked right at him. Owen's mind and body froze as he experienced the purest strain of terror of his life. Then the creature did something to his bewilderment: It began to retreat out of the mining site. A minute later its baleful glow had disappeared into the inky void of the ocean. Even Captain Harman sounded confused when he broadcasted once more.

"All hands and divers, stand down from alert status. The Leviathan is leaving. Report to your shift supervisors for further instruction."

Isaac beat Owen to the punch by radioing him first. "Team seven, the boss wants you back on the *Sequana* pronto. They need to know what you all were doing and what could have provoked such a targeted response from the rhadas towards that drone. Expect a lot of meetings and debriefs."

"Great, so I get to be locked up again," Owen grumbled back. "Why can't I catch a break?"

Owen spent the rest of the day rehashing the same story over and over. He lost track of how many different meeting rooms he'd had to sit in and absolutely none of the myriad of new people he had had to talk to. Scientist-types wanted him to provide insight on the mineral composition of the rock that the mining drone had been stuck in. Command-types wanted to know an aching blow by blow of the process team seven had taken right up until the Leviathan appeared. Everyone was trying to drill down to what had brought on the attack and why the Leviathan left so suddenly. Such things hadn't been observed before and thus warranted special attention.

As monumentous as the event had been, Owen was relieved when he was finally released back to his quarters and didn't have to relive the event for the hundredth time or get locked up. He was ready to collapse onto his bed and get what sleep he could before he had to be up for his usual shift in six hours. However, when his head hit the pillow and his eyes closed, the image of the Leviathan eye staring at him filled his mind. No amount of tossing and turning made the eye any less omnipresent. He told himself that this vision was just a fever dream brought on by the stress of the day's events. He tried to push the scene out of his mind's eye but the Leviathan remained in place. None of Owen's usual tricks for clearing his mind were working.

"Fine," he grumbled at the looming dream Leviathan. "I guess you can just float there and stare all you like. I'm going to get some sleep whether you like it or not."

[WHAT IS SLEEP?] the Leviathan said in a voice not unlike the memories of thunder Owen had from his childhood.

He wasn't expecting a reaction, which is why when the Leviathan *spoke* that he slammed his head against the ceiling when he bolted upright in bed. "You... talked?" Owen stuttered. "It wasn't enough that you're just a figment of my imagination going haywire. Now you have to torment me with words too?"

[WHAT IS IMAGINATION?]

"Great. My imagination is having an existential crisis. Just what I needed."

[WHAT IS IT YOU NEED?]

Owen started to reply something sarcastic but caught himself in time. Instead, he answered, "I need to stop hallucinating and dreaming about you. I need my life to get back to normal. Ever since you first started showing up my life's gone to shit."

[WE CAME IN ANSWER TO THE SUMMONS.]

"Summons? You're telling me that some part of me *wanted* this all to happen?" Owen scoffed. "I find that very hard to believe. Then again, I'm having a conversation with myself that would get me forced topside if anyone found out. Maybe I've had a screw loose longer than I thought."

[WHAT IS "TOPSIDE?"]

"You know, above the ocean. Past the ice ceiling. The surface."

[THAT CONNECTION IS WEAK.]

Owen wasn't quite sure what the dream Leviathan meant by that. Before he could start questioning it, though, a loud knock at his door woke him from his fugue state. He swung out of bed, opened the door to his quarters, and came face to face with Isaac. But Isaac wasn't alone. He had two burly security personnel with him.

"Hey boss," Owen yawned, thinking that this was just standard procedure whenever someone didn't report into work. "Don't tell me I overslept?"

Isaac's face twitched ever so slightly as he failed to maintain his poker face, the same tell that routinely cost him credits on game nights. "No. But I need you to come with us," he said stiffly.

"Cryptic, but alright," Owen commented as he quickly shimmied into rumpled clothing that was somewhat presentable. Then he stepped out of his quarters and motioned for Isaac to lead the way. The two security guards fell in step behind Owen, filling the corridor and preventing him from making a break for it.

Now fully awake, his mind raced as it tried to come up with reasons why any of this was necessary. Was the loss of that mining drone something like a "final strike" on his record? Especially since it brought on a literal Leviathan? Was this where he'd be told he was rotating topside whether he liked it or not? Did they expect him to resist or go on some kind of rampage?

No answer came to him. He just had to be patient and try not to panic. He could do that. Right?

CHAPTER 11

Thatch - E.F.S.V. Wolffish, Minos Mire

After three days of travel, Thatch and her crew aboard the *Wolffish* arrived at the new set of coordinates that O'Dea's "elderly acquaintance" had given them back at the Dark Lift. Initial scans weren't showing any kind of minable deposits, shipwrecks, or anything noteworthy. Rather than call it a wash, Thatch ordered a new tack.

"Switch from passive to active sensors," she ordered while in her command chair on the *Wolffish*'s bridge. "But keep power at 50% or lower."

"50% active scan, aye," Yukawa confirmed.

A loud, high-pitched ping known as the "Wolf Whistle" echoed through the ship as the *Wolffish*'s sensor suites barraged the surrounding waters and the ocean floor. The noise was both a consequence of going active and a warning to all aboard that such a change had occurred. Normally, one would want to remain as passive as possible when traveling and scanning. Going active revealed not just the *Wolffish*'s current position to every mercenary and pirate in the local area, but also could bring on a rhadas attack. The benefit of going active was a crystal-clear mapping of the surrounding waters down to even the smallest crevice and crack of the sea floor.

"Readings coming back now," Volodina reported as she read the incoming feeds of data. "Nearest rhadas swarm is fifteen clicks out. The seabed is unremark-- Hold on. I'm seeing a *massive* thermal vent approximately half a click to the northeast."

Thatch leaned forward as she asked, "A thermal vent? Why didn't passive sensors pick it up? Especially if it's of considerable size?"

Volodina studied the feeds, then responded, "From what I can tell it's situated in a small canyon, Admiral. The vent's deep enough that the water's the same temperature as the rest of the ocean by the time it's out of the ravine."

"Hm. It's been a long time since I plundered a thermal vent," Thatch mused to no one in particular. "Very well. This must be what that old man wanted us to see. Or, at least, that's what I'm going to choose to believe so that this trip has value. Enter into passive mode and take us over."

As the *Wolffish* moved into position, looming over the thermal vent like Luna over Earth, Thatch reviewed a mental checklist. Hydrothermal vents were more lucrative and perilous than usual mining. The slew of caustic chemicals and deadly heat they spewed into the ocean made approaching them a risk to begin with. Yet they contained crucial materials for life in the ocean. Europa's food chain started at the vents, where microbial life used chemosynthetic processes to produce food. These microbes in turn were fed upon by filter feeders and larger, shrimp-like creatures that had tough shells to be able to survive so close to the vents. These extremophiles were then hunted by larger xenos, and so on and so forth, until one reached the omnivorous apex predators: Leviathans.

Dwellers of the Sea of Sarpedon relied on these vents for food supplies and for raw building materials. Wealthy and brave explorers of the depths would set up settlements and waystations around vents. And while larger rhadas and even Leviathans would visit the vents from time to time, they never attacked submerged buildings. That protection extended to any vessel that was docked with them, making underwater structures truly safe havens. The Light Side of Europa relied on that fact for a significant amount of tourism. What tourist would be able to resist possibly seeing a Leviathan without the risk of being eaten?

That was the Light Side. Here on the Dark Side of Europa, in the Alagonian Depths, the vents were used as secret bases and staging grounds for pirates and mercenaries. Dark facilities that only allowed someone entrance if they knew the right code response and had a proper IFF beacon. This vent was shielded by the natural terrain, making it a juicy offering. A base here would be extremely hard to pick up on passive sensors. And if someone did go active they'd be dealt with quickly either by weapon emplacements or the rhadas.

"We're here, Admiral," reported Yukawa. "Bringing up hull lights and camera feeds now."

Holodisplays flickered to life before Thatch. Each was a window into a world that few had ever truly laid eyes on. Dark columns of umber water vomited from the vent openings, clouding the surrounding water. Around these clouds were corals, tube-like plants, and a smattering of exotically-colored creatures of various sizes. All of the critters glinted in the light like the starry heavens.

"It's… beautiful," Volodina said in awe as her eyes darted between feeds.

"First time seeing one in person?" Thatch asked with a smirk.

"Yes, Ma'am. I always heard they were treasures, but not like this."

"Enjoy the view then," said Thatch. Then to Yukawa, she asked, "What are we getting on passives?"

Yukawa was quick to answer, as if anticipating her inquiry, "It's a type F6, Admiral. Could sustain all of the Dread Lurkers or make for one hell of a biomass cache."

"Surely we won't be destroying this… this masterpiece?" Volodina asked as she turned to Thatch, her eyes pleading. "That would be such a waste."

"We could do with a proper base," Thatch replied wistfully. "It would be nice to have a port of call other than the Dark Lift. And it would be much, *much* cheaper in the long run to be able to repair our own ships and equipment. We'd still have to escort shipments back to the Dark Lift, but I think it's fairly clear that we have to capitalize on this opportunity. Start full survey operations and site marking. I'll get in touch with the other Captains."

She stood but stopped in the middle of her rise as another Wolf Whistle echoed across the ship. "Please tell me that was one of you hitting the wrong button by accident."

Yukawa's eyes widened as he glanced between Thatch and his readouts. "No, Admiral! I'm reading ten *Agunua*-class escorts closing in on our position! Their torpedo tubes are flooding and their arms are deploying!"

Thatch wasted no time in sitting back down and calling up the chair's VR interface. A bowl-shaped hood rose from the back of the chair, settled atop her head, then displayed the surrounding sea in real time. Haptic-feedback controls emerged from the chair's armrests, as well as pedals at her feet. She confirmed in an instant what Yukawa had reported. Ten small submarines, each a sixth the size of the *Wolffish*, were bearing down on her in circular formation. Their small articulating arms (two per vessel) were deployed and their attached weaponry glowing orange-hot.

"So, this was a trap then," Thatch sighed, yet followed it up with a chuckle. "Pretty ingenious of them. Get us trusting some old man that leads us to a big score, then lure us out of the way to raid us."

Volodina nervously asked, "What are we going to do, Captain? The *Wolffish* can't outrun *Agunua*-classes. Nor do we have enough firepower to take on ten at once on our own."

Though her face was obscured by the VR display, Thatch still grinned. "It's not about the level of firepower you have. It's how you use it. Taking full control of helm and offensive systems now. All hands, ready for boarders and repair operations!"

CHAPTER 12
Valentina - Midnight Hearts Mining Site, Carnus Expanse

Another long work shift passed for Valentina the day after the most recent xenos attempt at an incursion. She spent the initial hours on edge, half expecting the warning klaxon to go off at any moment. Yet the most notable thing to happen during the shift was when her cargo lifter's music system turned on by itself and began blaring Europa-local tunes by a group known as the SWL Project. Their music ranged from ambient electronica to more hardcore drum and base, but the one thing that remained constant regardless of how heavy the base was the inclusion of ice singers, which she had learned about from Mouse only a few days ago. Ice singers were a special type of Europan instrument that relied on carefully-cut ice being vibrated at just the right frequency. The result was an eerie, yet soothing, sound that worked great for this type of music. Valentina caught her foot tapping more than once to the rhythmic beat.

Valentina ended her shift by bringing the cargo lifter into the underground depot. The depot was carved from the ice crust into a vast open space with regular columns and breathable atmosphere. Valentina's understanding was that this was so the site's mining equipment could be serviced, no matter the size, without needing to worry about the air supply of any technicians.

However, in the few weeks she'd worked here, she had not seen, nor heard, of a single repair or service call that required bringing anything down into the depot. All repair work was done on location. Even when Min smashed the front of a cargo lifter in an accident a few days ago, the mechanics worked on the vehicle where it stopped.

The depot only saw use during shift changes to hand off vehicle controls. In Valentina's mind, this was a tremendous waste for the size of the pressurized underground area. Something more was at play here, though Valentina only had a few ideas as to what. The best theory she'd had was that there were levels of the compound that the average miner wasn't allowed to access or know about.

Waiting for her in the depot was the usual crew of Mouse, Min, and Hunzuu. Valentina toggled off the cargo lifter right as the dreadful three wails and two chirps echoed throughout the mining site. The boom of an explosion followed, shaking the ground, dimming the lights, and causing the carved ice walls in the depot to groan under the strain.

"Come on, boss lady," shouted Mouse as Valentina hopped out of the lifter. "This sounds super serious for once."

"If it's dire enough to make you not crack jokes, then it must be quite serious," Valentina said as the four of them ran for the nearest exit along with the rest of the miners in the space. But before they could make it halfway across the depot towards an airlock, another explosion sent them all stumbling.

"We may wish to think about securing ourselves in one of the vehicles here," Hunzuu called as he picked himself up. "I do not believe we will be able to make it to a bunker."

Min readily agreed, "Another explosion or two like that and we're going to lose pressure down here. We need to get into a vehicle ASAP."

Valentina concurred. She sized up what vehicles were nearby. Like her small group, the other individuals in the depot had either opted to keep running for a bunker or started sealing themselves into self-sustaining vehicles. That reduced the viable options down to a pair of sealed, nimble snowmobiles and a slow transport similar to the one that had brought them all out to the mining site to begin with. She weighed her options, and went with her gut:

"Into the transport there!"

Once inside, Valentina swung into the cockpit and fired up the controls. Soon breathable air circulated throughout the interior just as a third explosion caused a cave-in. Parts of the ice ceiling fell and crushed several rows of vehicles as the depot's air rushed out of the new hole. The ceiling debris was followed down by two xenos, ones Valentina recognized rapidly by the way they limped and bore scars on one side. These were part of the scouting party yesterday. This time they'd brought the full pack.

"Hang on to something!" she yelled, engaging manual control and steering the transport towards an auxiliary exit.

Valentina gave the transport all the gas she could, but their ride wasn't as fast as anyone aboard might have wished. The only saving grace was that the xenos did not care about them. Instead, they circled a patch of floor over and over. And when more xenos arrived via the hole they followed suit. Their numbers grew until twenty different xenos were present by the time Valentina's vehicle made it to an exit.

Valentina mentally-prepared to see devastation, but not on the level that awaited her. All the mining site's buildings had been ripped open or torn apart in a feral manner. Shards of metal, bone, and viscera from both injured xenos and unlucky miners littered the site as a few xenos continued to pick through the rubble. The mountainside was swarming with the creatures as well. Valentina expected to be spotted and meet a grizzly end.

Yet it never came. No xenos chased after her vehicle as it wound away from the mining site.

"I think we're in the clear!" cheered Mouse.

"Do not count your chickens before they hatch," cautioned Hunzuu. "We may be a snack they are saving for later."

"Oh, knock it off, Zuu," groaned Min. "Right now I'll take all the hope and optimism I can get."

Valentina interjected, "What are they doing? The xenos, I mean. I can only see so much up here while driving."

"I am unsure," Hunzuu began, then a vibrant flash of light filled the transport's cabin and shadowed the vehicle against the ice. "Although I am willing to wager that it has something to do with the column of light now pouring from the hole they made in the depot."

Indeed, there was a heavenly pillar coming from the ground when Valentina curved the vehicle so she could see via camera feeds on the side. "What the hell did we have down there?" she asked, half angry and half curious. "I can't think of what could be generating that light. Not even the nuclear reactors powering the site could produce that much energy."

"We could always turn around and go find out," Min sarcastically offered. "Does it matter though? We're escaping. Let the company deal with the aftermath. Our job now is to survive."

Silence fell for a time as all four of them realized the weight of that. Then Mouse exclaimed, "Ah man! This totally means we're not getting our paychecks this week!"
Valentina growled, "Someone take the wheel for a bit. I have to smack some sense into Mouse.

CHAPTER 13
Owen - E.S.V. Sequana, Alagonian Depths

Owen's nerves frayed like an overused cat scratching post. He'd been brought to the brig and placed in one of the cramped interrogation rooms. The table anchored to the floor and the two magnetic-grip chairs on either side of it took up most of the room. Owen wasn't claustrophobic but even he felt unnerved at the lack of space. Combined with how long he was left unattended, he felt lucky not to have a literal panic attack. The door to the room opened after what felt like an entire work shift had gone by.

"It's about ti--" Owen began to say, only to stop when he realized who was entering. He was expecting the Captain, Isaac, or maybe even Dr. Minerva. But Owen was not ready to see Skye with their hair up in a bun and wearing a lab coat.

"Hello, Owen," Skye said as they slipped into the opposite chair.

"How… Why are you here?" he asked, still flummoxed. "Since when are you with the science team?

Skye's neutral expression hardened as they replied, "Red Deck isn't the only place I work. Though I never thought I would be called upon for something like this. Much less that it would be you on the other side of the table."

Owen crossed his arms, leaned back in his chair, and frowned. "That's not cryptic at all. Why isn't anyone telling me what this is about?"

"I'm getting to that," Skye said in an attempt to soothe Owen's frustration. "First, some context. My field of expertise is xenopsychology, or the study of how aliens behave and how to predict what actions they might take. Normally, all I have to do is read what the *Sequana*'s sensors have picked up in regards to rhadas swimming patterns and compare it to what mining work is being done. Once I deliver a summary report that contains a prediction of how the rhadas will react, I don't have much to do but lurk on Red Deck."

"Well, I'll tell you what I told the other lab coats: I don't have any clue why that drone set off a Leviathan of all things," Owen sighed. "Or why the Leviathan just ate the drone and the drone alone before leaving. I've never seen anything like it before."

"Believe it or not, hun, you already know why the Leviathan did all that," Skye replied. "You just don't know that you know. Take a look at this."

Skye slid a holoslate across the table towards him. On it was replaying the footage from his pressure suit from back when he found that strange object putting out gamma radiation. It provided not just Owen's point of view but also a copious amount of recorded biosignals.

"Do you remember this?" Skye asked smoothly.

Owen barely glanced at the replay. "Pretty hard to forget. That's what landed me in the infirmary and off duty for so long. I assumed that Dr. Minerva saw this and that was why I ended up on 'vacation'. It's been weeks since then. Why is this important now?"

"At the time it was written off as just an oddity," Sky explained. "Follow-up visits to the location you found the object revealed zero signs that anything had ever been there besides Gadolinium. Nor did scans of your mind and body reveal any abnormalities. But look at this. This is a scan of your brain that was taken that day. And this is your brain as of the last scan taken earlier today before you left your pressure suit."

Skye tapped the holoslate and pulled up two images side by side. Both were colored impressions of what regions of the brain were active and how intensely. Though Owen had absolutely zero medical training, he could easily pick out that the most recent scan was awash with color compared to the rather dull result from the past.

"So what does this mean?" Owen said, meeting Skye's eyes for the first time since their arrival. "Is this why I've had all those hallucinations?"

"That's the thing, hun, they weren't hallucinations."

Owen threw up his hands as he scoffed, "Then what were they then? What else do you call a vision that isn't real?"

"They were real," asserted Skye as they tapped the display again. This time it showed footage of the Leviathan on one side and Owen's brain activity on the other. "Watch closely."

Owen did so, and his eyes widened. There was a spike in his brain activity right before the Leviathan showed up, and another in the moment where the beast decided to leave. And, instead of returning to normal, his brain activity remained severely elevated until he left his suit.

A ludicrous possibility occurred to him. Yet he wrote it off as fanciful thinking as he retorted, "I was afraid, in shock, and high on adrenaline. Doesn't everyone's brain do wacky things in such conditions?"

Skye shook their head. "Not at these levels. What I'm about to say will be stressful, hun. Please try not to panic. But after reviewing all the data on you and the rhadas, I can only come to one conclusion."

Owen tensed up and held his breath as Skye delivered their conclusion:

"Somehow, you are communicating with the xenos life in the surrounding area. And they are responding to your mental state. Perhaps even errant thoughts or passing wishes you experience in the moment."

Owen's entire body went numb as his vision began to tunnel. "No, that can't be possible. I can't actually be talking with the same mindless beasts that killed my dad."

[DO YOU NEED HELP?]

The sudden thunderous echo in his mind caused Owen to flinch. Something Skye picked up on in addition to Owen's body language.

"You're doing it right now, aren't you?" Skye asked cautiously. "Try to remain calm."

"No," Owen replied firmly, both in his mind and out loud. Then he continued in a raised voice, "How could anyone be calm after news like that?! Especially when I can see where this leads! Either you're going to force me to puppet these... these *things* or you're going to keep me locked away as a test subject for the rest of my life. Maybe even cut me up to get at the gooey bits!"

Skye tapped at the holoslate as they said, "I'm sorry, hun. But that's the situation you're in." Then they tapped more firmly. Owen's eyes fell upon the screen, which now had a message on it: *You need to get off the Sequana and either off world or to the Dark Lift. Those are the only two places you're going to be remotely safe.*

"And what am I supposed to do about it?" he asked, keeping up the charade for whomever was listening. He was still angry and resentful that Skye had kept such things from him, and that they were the ones delivering this news. But even he knew not to turn away a lifeline when it was offered.

"Just relax and stay calm," urged Skye as they typed another message. "There's no reason this has to be done the hard way."

This time the holoslate read: *If you can summon a Leviathan at 6400 hours, that's when your guard is being changed. I can maybe sneak you off the ship in all the confusion.*

"Fine," grunted Owen as he turned away from Skye. If the holoslate's chrono was correct, he had less than two hours to figure out how to summon a Leviathan but not kill everyone aboard the *Sequana*.

CHAPTER 14
Thatch - E.F.S.V. Wolffish, Minos Mire

The *Wolffish* banked hard up and to the right as Thatch performed a partial emergency ballast tank blow. Three torpedoes whizzed by and detonated against the sea floor as the *Agunua* wolf pack began to close in. The first of the smaller subs to come within grappling range tried a lateral cut with its vibrochainsaw across the *Wolffish*'s conning tower. Thatch rolled her ship so that it passed harmlessly above. Then she deployed one of the *Wolffish*'s six articulating arms. Specifically, the one with the pneumatic pile driver.

The *Wolffish*'s arm reached out and slammed the tip of the piledriver into the *Aguana*'s hull. A second later the massive metal spike punctured a hole clean through the smaller sub. Thatch tossed it aside and was forced into another ballast blow to dodge incoming torpedoes. She may have outskilled the captains surrounding her, as well as had bigger guns, but her assailants had the numerical advantage. Eventually Thatch would no longer be able to perform emergency ballast blows. And that would be when the circling predators would strike for real.

"Get me something to work with here!" Thatch shouted as she shook two more of the *Wolffish*'s arms free and batted some of the incoming projectiles away. This time their detonation could be felt throughout the ship.

"There is one thing we could try," Volodina offered with a hint of reluctance.

"There's no time for hesitation! Out with it!" ordered Thatch.

"We could use the vent," Volodina explained. "If we can lure the wolf pack into the plume and ignite it, the resulting explosion would probably wipe them out. Though it would also very likely destroy the vent in the process."

Thatch quickly replied, "Vents are replaceable. This ship and her crew are not! Yukawa, on my mark I want you to blow all the tanks. At the same time, launch a short fuse torpedo directly astern."

"Roger!"

The verbal exchange had cost the *Wolffish* two of its arms, plus a partially flooded deck from a glancing torpedo strike. But the *Aguana* wolf pack had also suffered thanks to Thatch's skills. Out of the original ten, one had been destroyed and three critically damaged. That left six destroyer submarines for Thatch to deal with. Not great odds, since for this plan to work she wouldn't be able to ballast blow again until the plan reached fruition.

"Incoming torpedoes, five o'clock!" called Yukawa.

"I see them! I see them!" yelled Thatch as she flooded the intercept torpedo tubes and launched a volley of counter-projectiles. While they blunted the blow, two enemy torpedoes still managed to slam into the *Wolffish*. The entire ship shuddered and multiple alarms blared as emergency bulkheads and doors slammed into place.

"Engine room 1 is flooded! And aft sensors are down!" reported Volodina, anticipating Thatch's request before it even had to be vocalized.

"Then we're going to have to eyeball this," growled Thrash.

She swung the *Wolffish* around, aiming right for the thermal vent's plume before dumping all available power into the remaining engines. Her sub surged forward, edging past another incoming torpedo volley with mere centimeters to spare. The six *Aguana* took the bait and chased after her.

"Come on… Come on…" whispered Volodina while Thatch executed another sharp roll.

Yukawa began to count down the distance before they hit the plume, "750 meters! 500! 400! 300! 200! 100! 50! Impact!"

Thatch's virtual reality display went dark as all visual feeds were obscured by the plume's gasses. She watched as the hull temperature rose to alarming levels. Even a sub like the *Wolffish* could only stay in such conditions for so long. She had to be absolutely sure the *Aguana* came in close enough to be affected by the potential blast. For that she relied on luck, and an active sonar ping.

"All hands, brace for impact!" shouted Thatch once all the targets were in the blast zone. Then she angled the *Wolffish*'s nose up forty-five degrees and gunned it. The instant the sub left the plume and visuals returned, she yelled at Yukawa, "Now!"

Five torpedoes dumped in the *Wolffish*'s wake from the rear tubes. They tumbled towards the plume, spooling up their detonation sequences. Once the torpedoes hit the black tower of smoke, they turned into miniature suns. The thermal vent amplified the explosions, devastating the surrounding area. Meanwhile the *Wolffish* rocketed upwards on the edge of the explosion.

For a moment Thatch worried that the ballast and the remaining engines wouldn't give her enough speed to save the ship. But then they crossed an ocean current. Not a particularly powerful one, but the water was flowing fast enough to disrupt the shockwave and redirect its compressive force long enough for the *Wolffish* to escape.

"Holy shit, it worked!" cheered Yukawa as Thatch disengaged from manual control. "That ought to send a strong message to whomever thought they could take on the Dread Lurkers!"

"But at what cost?" sighed Volodina as she tried to clear up the visual feed of what remained of the thermal vent. "There's no way we can make a base there now. And all that wildlife… Not to mention our own damage."

"If it means surviving another day, we take what we can get, Ms. Volodina," said Thatch firmly. "There will always be another thermal vent and another opportunity to put down roots. Until then, signal the *Tapti* and Captain O'Dea. We're going to need his help to limp back to the Dark Lift."

Yukawa spoke up hesitantly, "Er, Admiral. What if O'Dea was in on this whole debacle? Wouldn't calling him be a death sentence for us?"

"That's the chance we'll have to take, first mate. If he's nearby then we can reasonably assume that he's part of a conspiracy like you say. Otherwise, he has the only other submarine capable of defending us. I'd have to call half the Dread Lurkers fleet to match the *Tapti*'s firepower."

"Aye, Admiral," Yukawa said as he tried to remain stoic. "Sending the handshake signal now."

Half a minute later the image of O'Dea was being displayed on the largest of the *Wolffish*'s bridge screens. "How goes the search, Admiral?" O'Dea asked nonchalantly. "Judging by your expressions I'm going to guess it was a bust?"

"Worse, a trap," informed Thatch while she carefully took stock of O'Dea's facial expressions and tone of voice for any signs of treachery. "We made it out relatively intact, but I need you to come escort us on the way back to the Dark Lift."

O'Dea conferred with his bridge crew for a moment before replying, "We can rendezvous with you in a day and a half. Can you hold out that long?"

"We'll have to," sighed Thatch.

"Oh, and Admiral?"

"Yes, Mr. O'Dea?"

"I expect a bonus in this month's pay."

"Always money with you," Thatch observed. "But yes, you'll get something extra for this."

"Very good, *Tapti* out."

CHAPTER 15
Valentina - Somewhere in the Carnus Expanse

Long after the column of light from the former mining site vanished over the horizon, Valentina stopped the transport. After she joined the others in the back for a quick meeting.

"What have you all found that we can use?" Valentina asked as Hunzuu, Min, and Mouse added items to a pile between everyone.

"No food, but two bottles of water," reported Min sourly.

"I discovered two emergency pressure masks," added Hunzuu. "Each is good for 15 minutes of use."

Everyone turned to Mouse expectantly. He shrugged, still smiling as he produced a large caliber pistol and a four-inch knife. "Found these two hidden in the bathroom," he said jovially. "Rather odd place to keep them if you ask me. Though there was that one time when my third cousin--"

Valentina cut him off, "Alright so we don't have much. Keep the pistol for now, Mouse. You're the best shot among all of us, I think. I'll take the knife." Once the weapons had been secured, she continued, "We know it's a few days back to the Light Lift, so we're going to have to go hungry for a bit. But that's another problem. As far as I can tell, the autonav doesn't have any programmed coordinates or headings. Anyone happen to recall the general direction to the Light Lift?"

Silence fell as all racked their brains for an answer. Even Mouse's brow furrowed while his trademark smile disappeared. Hunzuu spoke up first, "I believe there's a mountain to the west that is relatively close to the Light Lift. Though I do not remember its name nor what degree of west it might be."

Valentina was glad she'd paid half-attention to that tour guide on the ride down from orbit. "We're looking for the Singate Massif then. That ring any bells for anyone?"

"Yeah!" exclaimed Mouse. "A friend of my brother's wife's uncle climbed it once! Said it was a breathtaking view."

"That's great, Mouse," interjected a sullen Min. "But it doesn't help *us*."

"Let me finish. He always said he particularly enjoyed seeing the contrast of the mountain against the border of the Brigid crater. And I know where that is roughly thanks to those Ice Hunters that rescued me when I crash landed!"

"I thought they were pirates," Min grumbled.

"I can't believe I'm saying this, but for once I think Mouse's story might help us," Valentina relented. "Unless anyone has a better idea, let's have Mouse take the wheel for a bit to get us going in the right direction. Then we can set up a rotation to keep us all frosty and not require us to stay up all day."

Mouse snapped a salute. "You got it, boss lady!"

Min didn't bother lowering her voice as Mouse clambered into the driver's seat. "And what's going to happen when it turns out like every other story he's told? That it's utterly made up and has more holes than swiss cheese? It's already bad enough we're stranded and lost. But at least we're close enough to the mining site that Midnight Heart rescue teams might find us. And what if he drives us into a cavi and we get stuck?"

"Then we'll freeze and die," Valentina said morbidly. "Just like if we sit here doing nothing waiting for a rescue that might never come. At least this gives us a chance of finding our way back before it's too late."

Min's expression declared that she wanted to protest further, though she simply let out a huff and went to sit by one of the transport's windows. Hunzuu and Valentina looked at each other. Hunzuu shrugged and sat across from Min. Valentina moved to the back of the transport, reclined a chair as far as she could, and tried to catch a quick nap.

Sleep came easier than Valentina expected, and soon she was experiencing anxiety-produced dreams full of swarming xenos and of her struggling to breathe. These nightmares teetered on the edge of waking her but never crossed the threshold. The only solace she had was that the xenos didn't have Wesler's face, like so many other specters in her night terrors.

After the sun had gone down and Europa was in Jupiter's shadow, Valentina awoke to a copper scent in the air. She rubbed the sleep out of her eyes and moved to where Hunzuu and Min had been earlier. They were still there but something was very wrong. Each was dead still with a bullet hole in their temples. Valentina also noticed the transport was no longer moving.

"Oh gods," she said as she tried not to throw up being in the presence of the deceased. "Mouse, please tell me you're still here?"

The sound of a hammer being pulled back on a gun came from behind her, followed by cool metal being pressed against her skull. "I am indeed, Ms. Kukleva."

The shock of hearing her real name was enough to snap Valentina out of feeling sick and into adrenaline-fueled hyperawareness. "How long have you known?"

"I had a hunch for some time, but I didn't know for sure until just now," Mouse said matter-of-factly.

"So, what then? You're going to kidnap me? Hold me for ransom?"

Mouse chuckled, "Oh no. Mr. Wesler was very clear on the matter. He wanted his songbird back intact. But nothing says I can't injure you in a non-permanent manner if I have to."

Valentina needed time to come up with a plan, so she stalled by asking, "How did you kill Min and Hunzuu without me noticing? I'm not that heavy of a sleeper. Were you also why the mining site got attacked by xenos?"

"The first is simple," Mouse responded proudly. "I had my own silenced pistol in addition to the one I found aboard. Quiet as a mouse, ironically enough. As for the xenos attack, no. That wasn't me. But it was a convenient stroke of luck that forced you out of the protection offered by the mining site."

"And how long have you been working for that bastard Wesler?" Valentina questioned in a bid for more time.

"About a week after your arrival to Europa. Don't worry, I handled all your loose ends," Mouse snickered. "All those people… Shame they had to be disposed of. All because you couldn't stay in your cage where you belonged. Wesler himself has come to Europa to see you back to Earth safely. There will be no escape for you. So just do as you're told and I won't have to break anything."

Valentina grunted as she finished taking stock of the situation. She still had the four-inch knife hidden up her sleeve, but to use it effectively she had to be quick, quicker than Mouse. And if she didn't pull it off that would be the end of her escape attempt. Yet she had no choice. She wouldn't return to Wesler. Not so long as she had any ability to fight back.

"You're right," she sighed, relaxing her shoulders. "I'll comply."

Mouse pulled the pistol back from her head and said, "Turn around, wrists up facing me."

She turned to see Mouse wearing an expression of contempt that was at such odds compared to how jovial he'd been up to this point. He had two guns pointed at her, the large caliber lower than the smaller one that had a silencer attached to its barrel. Next, she offered out her wrists while getting ready to slip the knife into her right hand.

The moment Mouse glanced away to put one of the pistols down, Valentina lunged at him. A gunshot wrang out as the two fell to the floor. Silence fell over the transport.

"Well… done…" gurgled Mouse.

Valentina's knife pierced Mouse's sternum and punctured his heart directly. Blood welled up and ruined the fabric across Mouse's chest as he took one final, shuddering gasp. Then there was stillness. The knife remained lodged in his chest as Valentina rolled off of him and backed away in horror. She'd never killed anyone before. Not even when getting away from Wesler. Now she had done what she prayed she never would have to. The worst part was how easy killing Mouse had been. How little resistance the knife offered as she severed his life line.

"Weinwurm was right," Valentina whispered, curling up into a ball and rocking back and forth. "I can't trust anyone but myself out here."

Unfortunately, Valentina's woes did not stop there. A low hiss emanated from the right wall of the transport. Breathable atmosphere was leaking out.

CHAPTER 16
Owen - E.S.V. Sequana, Alagonian Depths

Once Skye departed from the interrogation room, Owen closed his eyes and tried to make it seem like he was sleeping or otherwise waiting patiently. Beneath that facade he tried his best to reach out to the voice that belonged to a literal Leviathan. His first few attempts were nothing more than shouting at the void that lay beyond his mind. He knew there was no chance of getting off the *Sequana* without Skye's help, and to do that he had to ask *rhadas* for help. He struggled to push past the deep-seated hatred in order to work with beings that he'd hated and despised for almost half his life. Part of him almost *wanted* to be dissected or turned into a test puppet, that he might serve as a stepping stone to tormenting or defeating the rhadas. That inner turmoil made concentrating difficult for Owen. His turbulent emotional state bled through the link enough that the Leviathan noticed his attempts at communication.

[DO YOU NEED HELP?] the creature repeated in Owen's mind.

"First things first, I hate you," Owen thought-spoke back at the Leviathan. "I hate everything about you and your kind. You *took my father away from me* because you had to protect stupid fucking rocks. But as much as I wish I could tell you to piss off and never contact me again, I can't. I need your help getting out of here."

[WHAT IS HATE? WE ONLY PROTECT THE RUINS OF THE PROGENITORS.]

"I don't have time to explain basic damn emotions to you," snarled Owen. Though in his anger he felt no need to inquire about these "progenitors" he filed that away to ask about later. If there was a later. Then he continued, "I need you and however large enough swarms are out there to cause trouble for the *Sequana* and the defense fleet. But not by killing them."

[THE METAL CREATURES HARM AND KILL MANY OF US. WHY SHOULD WE NOT KILL THEM?]

"Because I'm not about to sacrifice hundreds of lives just to make an escape," Owen retorted without any hesitation. "I'm not a killer. I don't want that sort of thing on my conscience."

[WHAT IS 'CONSCIENCE?']

"For the love of… Can you do what I'm asking or not?"

[HARASSING METAL CREATURES WITHOUT KILLING THEM WILL MEAN MANY OF US WILL BE KILLED OR INJURED.]

Owen growled back, "I don't give a damn. You're disposable. Human life isn't. I ask again: Are you going to do it or not?"

[YES,] said the Leviathan simply.

Then the omnipresent eye and booming voice vanished from Owen's mind. His entire body filled with furious anger and painful stress brought on by unnecessarily-tensed muscles. A fire that refused to stop burning regardless of the consequences. His fury grew to the point that his balled fists and jaws ached and his stomach churned. Though that period of waiting helped Owen realize he wasn't just seething about the rhadas and his newfound connection to them. He was livid with Skye for living a double life that they never told him about. He was upset at the universe for knocking him down every time he got back up and started putting things back together. But most importantly, he was irritated with himself. That his bad luck and curious nature that landed him in this dreadful set of circumstances as an unwilling conduit for the rhadas.

Owen didn't have long to process these emotions and thoughts before a warning klaxon sounded across the *Sequana*. Loud shouting came from the other side of the door, followed by three booming crashes of metal. He rose and tensed himself up, ready for a fight. Then the door opened. Three burly guards were limp against the corridor walls and floor, blood pooling beneath them. Standing amid all of them was Skye clutching a nasty gash that had torn open their right forearm.

"How did you…?" Owen said as he joined Skye in the hallway. "Are they…?"

"Doesn't matter," Skye said through gritted teeth. "We have to get you to Landing Bay 4. I'm not going to be able to use this with my arm in this condition. Take it and keep it hidden until it's absolutely necessary to use it."

Skye handed Owen a pneumatic harpoon pistol, one of the few kinds of firearm that could be used on a submarine like this without having to worry about igniting the atmosphere or accidentally resulting in explosive decompression from a stray bullet. Owen had never used one before outside of the VR suites. He started to reject it, only for Skye to cut him off and shove the weapon into his hands.

"We don't have time for this! Take the damn thing and let's go!" Skye shouted at him before moving down the corridor.

Owen followed best he could as the deck shifted and bucked from what he assumed were evasive maneuvers to avoid rhadas attacks. He and Skye made their way through several decks without incident thanks to all the chaos and confusion. But once they made it to the deck containing the landing bays, a security guard stopped them.

"What happened to your arm?" the man asked, hand already on the baton hanging from his belt.

"Fell into a desk corner," Skye answered, not having to fake the pain they were in. "Gotta get to the infirmary."

"You're going the wrong way," insisted the guard. "Sick bay is two decks up and towards the stern. This just leads to the landing bays."

Skye looked back at Owen and gave a slight nod. Owen started to pull up the pneumatic pistol with a trembling hand only to have to abort to catch himself when the *Sequana* lurched to the side and pitched violently. Skye fell on their injured arm, while the guard slammed his head into an exposed pipe. Both cried out in pain, though only Skye remained conscious as Owen found his feet again. He kneeled next to Skye, unsure of where to touch or how to try and help them up.

"Go," Skye grunted, pointing with their blood-coated free hand towards the landing bay. "There's a Class-V personal transport in slot 3. Access code is 23187. Don't tell me where you're headed. Just go."

"But I can't just leave you here," protested Owen. "Come on, we can get there together."

Skye coughed up blood as they grabbed Owen by the collar. "I'm in no shape to take up half the air and space in that transport. As much as I would like to come along to pick your brain about the rhadas, I have to stay here. Face the consequences."

Owen's body went cold as he retorted, "You know what they'll do to you when they find out you let me out, right?"

"Doesn't matter," insisted Skye. "Now go! Don't look back!"

Owen lingered in hesitation before rising and starting to walk away from Skye towards the landing bay. Or so he forced himself to believe in an attempt to not seem like a coward. The truth was Owen scrambled as fast as he could without looking back. He angled straight for the third vehicle slot once inside, and sure enough there was a cigar-shaped two-man transport usually meant for day-tripping VIPs. The access code got him inside as the *Sequana* creaked dangerously. The transport had little interior space. Owen had to crawl in and sit leaning forward in a prone position, with barely enough headspace to glance about the transparent front of the vehicle. Once the hatch was sealed, he keyed in an emergency sequence that dumped him beneath the *Sequana* into the ocean.

The reason for the *Sequana*'s sudden movements and warning noises was apparent. A Leviathan had coiled around the submarine several times, locking it in place. Sonic blasts and anti-rhadas torpedoes pecked at the creature, yet it remained unflinching. One of the rhadas' eyes looked down towards Owen's vehicle.

[RUN,] the Leviathan said in Owen's mind.

"I'll need a smokescreen of some kind," he ordered.

Moments later, a swarm of medium-sized rhadas surrounded his transport. They moved with him as he angled away from the *Sequana* and out of the mining site while other swarms harassed the defense fleet and continued the distraction.

Owen pulled up the rear camera feed and took one last glance at his former home. Then he called the rhadas off. Thankfully, they listened, and soon he was lost in the depths alongside them. To what end he wasn't sure. But he knew he couldn't squander the opportunity Skye had given him.

CHAPTER 17
Valentina - Somewhere in the Carnus Expanse

"Where in the hell are you?!" Valentina shouted as she performed another pass of her transport's wall in search of the hole leaking precious air. She could find no obvious bullet hole, and no amount of straining her ears helped. Her heart raced and she broke out in a cold sweat as she glanced at the pressure readout in the cockpit to gauge how much time she had left. There wasn't much: A few hours at best. After that she'd lapse into unconsciousness as the available oxygen in the vehicle finished escaping.

Out of desperation, Valentina reengaged the transport's motors and set the autopilot to continue on the path that Mouse had set them on before his betrayal. She realized that she could be driving into a trap set by Wesler, but she preferred that over dying a slow death gasping for air, though not by much. If an ambush or a random passerby wasn't waiting somewhere on the horizon then all anyone would find is the transport with four dead bodies in it.

Valentina moved the corpses of Min, Hunzuu, and Mouse to the back left side in order to search for the leak. She tried to be as respectful of the dead as possible, though they were still piled up unceremoniously thanks to the cramped nature of the transport. She couldn't bring herself to touch them again to put them in more dignified positions. That she had been able to move them in the first place, let alone touch them, was a small miracle. She'd seen death like this before during her past life on Earth, but had never dealt with the cleanup.

That she had formed a blossoming friendship with the deceased wasn't helping matters either. Min was always the sour pessimist, and Hunzuu was the strong silent type. Neither deserved to die, much less because of Valentina. She kept mentally repeating what Mouse had said about disposing of "all those people" in "tying up loose ends." Did that mean the kindly woman who did her hair was dead? What about the man who interviewed her for the Midnight Hearts? Or even that Ice Hunter, Weinwurm, she'd received help and advice from? Was their blood all on her hands as well?

She nearly gave over to despair and fatigue. Yet Valentina kept searching for the leak. If she stopped now, she realized that she wouldn't have the strength to do anything else. By focusing on this one crucial task she pretended that there was still hope. Too bad hope wouldn't let her breathe. Nor would it wash away her guilt.

A low oxygen alert started to sound before Valentina knew it. She was beginning to find it difficult to breathe, lapsing in and out of consciousness. By sheer luck she found the bullet hole between fade outs. Though it was probably too late, she still managed to fight for awareness long enough to plug the hole with emergency sealant. After that everything swirled to black.

How long Valentina remained in that state of limbo was unclear. All she knew is that a familiar voice broke the void's silence, though in her present state the sounds were all muddled together. She lacked the energy and will to open her eyes. Yet she was breathing easily enough. That meant someone had found her. Whether or not it was the right type of someone she wasn't sure. The need to determine which drove her to concentrate on trying to figure out who it was that was talking.

"...that's when I moved her to my sled and came back here," said the voice, now distinguishable as belonging to a man. "She's been out cold for a full day."

Another voice, this time a woman's soprano being fed over a radio, replied, "And what will you be doing with her? That Wesler guy has put up a very public bounty for whomever brings her in alive. There's enough zeros at the end of the credits reward that nearly all of Europa is going to be looking for her."

"Then I guess I'll have to take her to the Dark Side," returned the man. "With any luck, one of my old connections will be able to take her in and keep her safe."

The woman sighed, "You're going to toss her to the lurkers of the dark? Wouldn't they leap at the opportunity to claim such a bounty?"

The man answered, "Not this one. She's one of the rare few on this cursed moon that has a moral code and the means to protect it."

"So be it. As promised, I won't breathe a word of this to anyone. But you owe me big for this, Weinwurm."

As the woman's voice faded, Valentina focused on the last word. She knew the name Weinwurm, but from where? Her muddled brain struggled to return to full processing power. In a flash of inspiration, she connected the dots. He was that Ice Hunter on the *Arcadia*.

"Weinwurm," Valentina groaned as she tried to open her eyes. They resisted her efforts at first, but once open they behaved. Several long blinks later and the blurry environment around her came into focus. She was in a survival tent, a specialized, portable dome used as a temporary shelter against the elements for Ice Hunters and the odd group camping out on the ice fields of Europa.

The hardened face of Weinwurm came into Valentina's field of view. "Welcome back," he said cautiously. "Take it easy. You were barely hanging on in low atmo when I found you. I don't believe you'll have any permanent brain damage, but best not to push things right away. Do you remember who you are, who I am?"

"I'm... Valentina Victorovna," she answered slowly. "You're Weinwurm, an Ice Hunter. How did you find me?"

"Luck mostly," he admitted as he offered her a drink from a water bottle. She took the guided sip as Weinwurm explained further, "I was out hunting for someone when I saw your transport doing donuts next to a ravine. Naturally I went to help. Imagine my surprise when my target was dead inside with you next to the body. Did you become an Ice Hunter when I wasn't looking?"

"No, no just a miner," Valentina clarified. Then she guessed, "Was your target the one with the knife in his chest?"

Weinwurm nodded back. "Yep. Wanted for dozens of murders and various other crimes. He was the type of merc that didn't deserve the title of Ice Hunter. Not even 'assassin' fit his crimes. He was a chaotic element that left a trail of blood in his wake."

"Fucking Mouse," swore Valentina. "And to think he had me believing his wild stories at the end. He apparently had been tailing me looking for an opportunity to turn me in to Wesler. And from the sounds of it Wesler came all the way out here to Europa. Why aren't you worried about him?"

"Heard that conversation did you," chuckled Weinwurm. "To be honest, credits don't do it for me any longer. I have enough saved up that I could retire to some cushy estate in Mars' orbit. Now I do what I do out of a desire to see a better Europa in the future. Even if this frozen hell keeps trying its damnedest to kill me."

Valentina processed that for a moment before asking, "And you're okay with the chance that Wesler might put a bounty on you as well if he finds out you helped me?"

"I'm not concerned about that," he grinned back. "You can throw all the money you want at a problem here on Europa, but it won't change how brutal the ice and the ocean is. Sure, some might try and take me down. Yet in all my years no one's come close to accomplishing it."

"I see," she sighed. "Who's this person you're taking me to meet on the Dark Side?"

"I think you'll like her. Her name's Thatch, and…"

CHAPTER 18
Thatch - Dark Lift

"Let's make sure I have this all correct," Admiral Thatch said as she thumbed through the stack of reports once more in her Ready Room. She'd brought the *Wolffish* back to the Dark Lift in one piece (more or less) and was now dealing with the repair efforts. "Engine room 1 will need to be completely replaced, including the driveshaft. The breached sections of Deck 2 can be drained and inspected, but you're recommending a complete replacement of half that deck. Why is that, Mr. Haar?"

Haar was a grizzled man with a beard and face that were both weathered from "blue collar" experience. When he spoke via the holoscreen it wasn't with the sleazy tone that salesmen relied on to make dishonest commissions. Instead, his manner of speaking was direct and matter-of-fact. "Simply put, you've got some crucial wiring running through the aft section of Deck 2. We're talking arm and rudder control, in addition to ballast tanks three through seven. A simple drain and inspection might not catch all potential issues. My team and I are great at what we do, but I've seen this sort of thing before at least twice. In those cases it led to those subs not coming back."

His expression softened as he added, "There's also something to be said of the smell. Unless you replace the whole thing, there's always going to be a hint of mildew clinging to that part of Deck 2."

That got Thatch to genuinely laugh, "Very well! The *Wolffish* is the closest thing I'll likely have to a child, so it's only natural for me to splurge a bit to see her repaired properly. Is your original estimate here of three weeks correct?"

Haar nodded in reply, "We're looking at roughly 1,700 hours of work. That'll include restocking your armaments and other supplies. Hope you don't mind hanging out here at the Dark Lift."

"I can think of worse places to have a stopover," she joked back. A quick signature and document transfer later and she added, "There you are, Mr. Haar. You may begin work at your earliest convenience. I will have the crew remain out of the way. Should you need anything immediate, please reach out through my first officer, Mr. Yukawa. He'll be remaining aboard for the full duration."

"You got it. Dock Logistics out."

Once the comm link terminated, Thatch called in Yukawa to her Ready Room. He wasted no time in entering and standing at parade rest. "Yes, Admiral?"

"I'm putting you in charge of overseeing the repair efforts," ordered Thatch with a smile. "Haar says it'll take three weeks, more or less. Think you can handle that?"

Yukawa beamed appreciatively as he said, "Of course, Admiral! I won't let you down!"

"See that you don't, Mr. Yukawa. Along that same line, I'll be involved in several meetings over the next few days with the Grand Admiral and some of the other Admirals currently in port. A proper security detachment will accompany me, of course, but it does mean I will be unavailable for long stretches of time."

"Understood, ma'am," Yukawa answered with a slight bow. "Is there anything else?"

"Not at this time. You're free to go."

Yukawa saluted then promptly departed. That left Thatch to prepare for the first of the meetings. The importance of meetings involving other Admiralty made it vital that Thatch both looked and performed her best. There would be all manner of hidden agendas and politicking that Thatch would have to suss out and stay on top of. Otherwise, she could end up with both a metaphorical and a literal knife in her back. But that's what made the Grand Admiral's meetings so much fun for Thatch. Better to be constantly reading the room than to be stuck nodding off while Admirals droned on.

The process of getting dressed in perfectly presentable fashion took several hours before Thatch was finally content enough to actually leave the *Wolffish*. Thirty minutes later saw her joining four other Admirals and Grand Admiral Triton in the Grand Admiral's shrine above the ice. Thatch only roughly knew the names of the other Admirals and what faction they represented. Triton began the meeting before small talk could be made with any of them.

"Let's get right to the point," Triton said as he conjured up a holodisplay of a Leviathan coiled around a C&C submarine typically used by mining companies on the Light Side. "This is footage of the *E.S.V. Sequana* taken a week ago. Watch carefully."

Thatch and the other Admirals watched as the Leviathan and other rhadas swarms made a mess of things for the miners. Each was expecting to see the *Sequana* crushed like a tin can, and were therefore shocked when the Leviathan released the submarine and left the area. One of the other Admirals spoke up first:

"In all my years, I've never heard of a Leviathan giving up that easily," commented Admiral Rogier, a stout man whose belly strained against the fabric of his golden uniform. He represented the Golden Bones, a group similar to Thatch's Dread Lurkers in the operations they undertook and the respect they commanded. "Is this some kind of new weapon or deterrent?"

"If it is, it has evaded all of my intel networks," chimed in Admiral Serenity. Her immaculate gray uniform represented the Frozen Shadows. They were best known for their information trading network that spanned all of Europa from high in orbit down to the deepest depths. "And I don't need to stress how impossible that is."

"There's always a first time for something," Admiral Kahn teased. Of all the Admirals present, he looked the most disheveled. He and his Bottom Feeders weren't the most glamorous of factions, usually feeding off the scraps and less-than-savory tasks other factions wouldn't touch.

The Grand Admiral cleared his throat, "Be that as it may, this represents a major shift in what we know about the rhadas. This mining company, the Blue Bison Mining Consortium, isn't sharing any details. The only reason I received this footage in the first place is due to an old friend of mine with the defense fleet leaking it to me directly. Otherwise, the entire incident would have been swept under the rug like it was nothing. Still probably will be, unless I or one of you leaks this."

"Then that suggests it is indeed a new weapon they tested, as Rogier proposed," observed Thatch. "What do you want us to do, Grand Admiral? I can certainly commit part of my fleet to an assault if you wish, though the *Wolffish* herself is currently being repaired."

Thatch had deliberately voiced this proposal. Everyone present knew that she called in the rest of the Dread Lurkers fleet to protect the *Wolffish* until it was fixed. By offering to send some away, she left a potential opening for others to strike. Admitting such was a test of sorts, one that Admiral Kahn failed when his sly grin briefly became a frown. The slipup wasn't a full admission that he and the Bottom Feeders were behind the attack at the vent, but it gave Thatch a thread to investigate further after this meeting.

"I do not believe an assault is necessary," waved off Triton. "However, I want it to be made crystal clear that whoever discovers the secret of this event will be handsomely rewarded, on the condition that they share their findings with all factions operating out of the Dark Lift. I am not about to allow an arms race, is that clear?"

Thatch and the other Admirals all voiced their consent. Triton nodded before pulling up a new holo image. This time the image was of an Earth nobleman and a girl that looked native to Europa. "Next is this fellow. This man here is Rolf Wesler," Triton explained. "Apparently his bride, Valentina, ran to this moon to escape her marriage. Wesler is offering an exuberant sum to anyone that brings Valentina back to him intact. Normally I wouldn't mention such a thing to you all, but I believe we must present a unified front. He believes that by throwing credits around that he can command the services of anyone on Europa. We need to commit that, should Valentina appear at the Dark Lift or if you discover her in your travels, the Dark Lift will not turn her over. In other words, I am extending my personal protection to this woman."

The one remaining Admiral who hadn't spoken until now stepped forward. From what Thatch knew, Admiral Chen and her Crimson Serpents worked closely with Ice Hunters for jobs like the one this Wesler character was offering. They also handled special Dark Side security details from time to time. "I will inform my agents immediately, Grand Admiral," Chen said with a slight dip of her head. "You can be assured that she will arrive here unharmed should she take an overland route."

Kahn crossed his arms and grumbled, "I don't see why we're giving this girl special protection. What makes her so important and worth throwing away that many zeros for?"

"If you were paying attention, the Grand Admiral just said it was because he willed it to be so," Serenity sighed. "However, I do also know from my network that she is an heiress to a major Earth-Luna logistics faction."

"The top brass here wants another logistics type on his side," chortled Rogier, causing his belly to jiggle. "No offense, Grand Admiral, but that does track."

"None taken," Triton replied. "My belief has always been that logistics, not might, is how one controls and manages any port of call. Firepower alone cannot repair ships or trade goods. I simply wish to have a conversation with Ms. Valentina and pick her brain. With that said, I have no further items of discussion for today. You may leave."

Each Admiral bowed and returned to the lifts. However, rather than go all at once, they staggered such that only two were in a lift at a time. Thatch deliberately paired herself up with Serenity on the ride down.

"What else do you know about this Valentina?" Thatch asked directly. "You don't normally give such context for free, even to the Grand Admiral."

Serenity turned slightly to reveal a frown. "Let us say that her circumstances remind me of how my family first came to Europa. I have been following her since Wesler first arrived at the Light Lift. That is all I can say for the moment."

"Fair enough," grunted Thatch as she crossed her arms. "To be honest I'm far more concerned about this new weapon that drives off Leviathans. That kind of technology could change the entire balance of the Sea of Sarpedon. Why would some random mining company have such a thing?"

"I don't know," Serenity admitted. "But you can be damn sure I *will* find out."

CHAPTER 19
Owen - Somewhere in the Minos Mire

With no specific destination in mind, Owen had stayed with the rhadas swarm as it wandered about the ocean. Their journey took him past multiple thermal vents where the rhadas stopped to feed and otherwise rest. Even the Leviathan that Owen had been talking to lingered instead of moving on. Owen's transport had thrown up so many alarms due to the creatures that he had to shut off most proximity sensors and then pilot without greater knowledge of his surroundings.

An abnormal glow from the seafloor caught his eye on the third day. "What on the moon is that," he asked as he angled the transport down to get a better look. The light was beaconing out from within a deep canyon filled with thermal vents. Between the vents were crystalline structures. Owen swore he could pick out roads and buildings as he got closer. However, before he entered into the canyon proper, the Leviathan swam in front of him.

[THIS IS A NEST,] it explained. [DO NOT DISTURB IT.]

"You mean to say this is where rhadas like you come from?" asked Owen via their mind-link. "Are these ruins of the 'Progenitors' that you're protecting?"

The Leviathan simply repeated, [THIS IS A NEST. DO NOT DISTURB IT.]

"Alright, I get it. I was just curious," sighed Owen as he glanced at the transport's status readout. "Not that it matters. I've got maybe two days of air left tops. I have no idea where I am in relation to either the Light or the Dark Lift. Chances are that I'll die in this coffin."

[DO YOU REQUIRE HELP?]

"Unless you can somehow get me close enough to civilization without tripping any warnings so I can pretend I was running from you, not really. I've more or less accepted my fate at this point."

The Leviathan opened its maw wide, and for a moment Owen thought that this was its way of mercy-killing him. Instead of biting down around him, though, the creature kept its mouth ajar. [WE CAN CARRY YOU TO A METAL RING.]

"You want me to ride in your mouth?" Owen said, disgusted and unnerved. "I guess I don't have much choice, do I? Either I rely on your speed and knowledge of Europa's ocean, or I die in the dark. Or you'll just decide to eat me halfway towards wherever it is you want to take me."

[YOU HAVE BEEN BLESSED BY THE PROGENITORS. YOU ARE NOT TO BE EATEN.]

"Well, that's a relief," Owen commented sarcastically. "Fine. Whatever. Let's do it."

With that he carefully guided his transport around the Leviathan's deadly teeth to float above its barbed tongue. The mouth slowly closed around him, yet the expected swallowing motion did not follow. Instead, Owen felt a shift in momentum as the Leviathan started swimming off to an unknown destination at terrifying speed. All he could do was sit and watch the clock count down until his air supply ran out. For once in his life, instead of feeling nervous or dread, Owen accepted the fact things were out of his control.

That revelation didn't hit Owen until several hours of travel passed. Most of his formative years had been spent trying to stay within the structure and relative safety that came with underwater mining: show up on time, never waste a moment while on shift, don't be dead weight or drag others down, that sort of thing. But like most life-changing events on Europa, all it took was one chance encounter to cause nine years of his life to be tossed aside. That the rhadas both started and ended his problems was bitterly ironic.

Owen continued pondering that notion. From the sounds of things, this mental connection he had with the rhadas, this so-called "blessing of the progenitors," wasn't going to disappear any time soon, if at all. That meant he'd either have to hide such powers indefinitely, leave Europa entirely, or throw his lot in with an unsavory dark side faction. The former two were easier said than done. He couldn't touch his account of saved credits without giving away his position. And it was a sure bet that *someone* from the *Sequana* would come hunting to get him back. Owen supposed that only made sense. The ability to control and communicate with the rhadas could revolutionize how life on Europa worked, not just in the ocean but even on the surface as well. Whomever controlled him would be given a golden ticket to shape the future of the moon however they liked.

[WE ARE HERE,] the Leviathan announced as it opened its maw to permit Owen to leave.

"Thanks, I guess," Owen said as he risked turning on long range sensors. Besides the frantic alert that he was close to a Leviathan, his stolen transport picked up a thermal vent up ahead with a settlement around it. He had no idea what the settlement's name was, nor who controlled it. His current air supply meant he had little choice. He had to dock and pray that he came up with a plan before he was found out.

Once the Leviathan disappeared into the inky darkness of the sea without further comment, Owen angled his ride towards the settlement at full speed. The settlement consisted of three domes: one for docking/repair work, one for farming, and one for habitation. Geothermal power conduits connected the domes to the thermal vent below, while over half of the vent's emissions fed into the second dome to produce foodstuffs and other vital materials. No obvious markings were present on the dome to indicate affiliation with a specific faction, nor were the domes transparent like light side tourist traps. He was flying in blind, though he was noticed and hailed before he got too close to the docks.

"This is Oasis Station," radioed a man's voice with a note of concern. "You picked one hell of a time to stop by. We picked up a Leviathan not too long ago."

"That's what I'm running from, actually," replied Owen before transitioning into his imagined cover story. "I think I might be the last survivor from my group. It's a miracle I managed to escape the bastard and make it this far. Am I allowed to dock?"

"Clearing you for dock 7E now. What name should I put on file?"

Owen had no desire to return to this transport unless it was absolutely necessary. He gave a fake name, "Mr. Smith, if you would."

"As you wish. Someone will meet you at the umbilical to handle paperwork and any concerns you have. Welcome to Oasis Station."

Twenty minutes later Owen left the confines of the transport and stepped onto solid ground. Just as traffic control had said, a pencil-pusher was waiting for him. Owen continued his cover story across all documents - how he was the last known survivor of a small operation and how he likely would have to do a few odd jobs to cover docking fees. Each moment tested Owen's patience and ability to stick to a lie. He had to fight against becoming flustered so as not to cause suspicion. The process took almost an hour before Owen was allowed to travel throughout the station freely. His first order of business was a shower, followed by finding food.

The search for a meal brought him to an establishment that had no name, only a rusted bucket above the door. A dive bar similar to those on Red Decks by the looks of it, with a jukebox playing slow jazz. What patrons were inside paid Owen no mind as he slid into a seat at the bar and watched the holoscreens anchored into the ceiling. He looked for any news or hints about how his escape was reported. Assuming, of course, the event was disclosed at all. He made his way through a hearty meal and still nothing had appeared about the *Sequana* or any odd Leviathan attacks.

When the subject of the bill came up with the barkeep, Owen sighed and said, "I probably should have mentioned this sooner, but I don't exactly have a bunch of credits on me. Maybe I can work in the back to work the bill off?"

The barkeep started to reply in annoyance only as a booming voice interrupted them. "No need, my young friend! I will gladly cover it for you!"

Owen turned to see a shorter man with a worn-out, trench coat-like jacket and an all-too-eager smile. "That's very kind of you," Owen said. "But I don't have any way to repay you."

The man slid into the seat next to Owen, slapping down some credits for the barkeep before saying, "You can repay me by telling how you escaped a Leviathan! Very few can boast that feat, and fewer still could manage it in a Class-V transport."

Owen shrugged in what he hoped was a convincing manner. "Not much to tell, really. When I realized my ship was going down, I ran for the nearest ticket out of there. After that all I did was play cat and mouse with the rhadas. Lots of waiting, powering down, short sprinting, that sort of thing. I nearly ran out of air before I got here."

"I see, I see," said the man as he rubbed his chin. "That means you're lucky. No offense meant! I could use that kind of luck. And from the sounds of things, you could use a job."

"What do you have in mind," Owen asked cautiously. He was still feeling the weight of having his trust betrayed back at the *Sequana*, but something about this man's voice was inviting, confident, and made Owen feel like he was important.

"Allow me to tell you all about the Bottom Feeders…"

CHAPTER 20

Valentina - Somewhere in the Carnus Expanse

The overland journey to the Dark Lift with Weinwurm taught Valentina several valuable skills. Things like how to use the cover of ravines to hide from xenos, how to cold start an engine without any atmosphere, and how to purify and melt Europa's ice into drinkable form. Her training regimen with the Midnight Hearts Mining Corporation had touched on some of those important lessons but ended up skipping over practical demonstration and practice in favor of focusing on mining equipment use and maintenance. These lessons included stories from Weinwurm as the two sped along the ice.

"...and that's why you should always take the third card from the left," finished Weinwurm. "Unless you want to be out a few thousand credits."

"Xenos Gambit sounds like such a silly game," Valentina commented as she rode in tandem on Weinwurm's snowmobile. The vehicle was Europan-standard with three motorized, spiked treads and an enclosed space half the size of the transport she was rescued from. "It has more bluffing than what I recall of Poker, but it's not nearly as reliant on counting cards or the luck of the draw. In fact, it sounds like most hands are predetermined the moment they're dealt. I guess you have to excel at deceiving others to make it more than a few rounds with your wallet intact. One small slip up and it's over."

"You catch on quickly," said Weinwurm. "That need of a poker face and importance on appearance is why it's so favored among those that use the Dark Lift as a port of call. Well-to-do Captains and Admirals peacock around the place, assuming that their emblems, colors, and fine clothing means you're able to tell who to avoid and who might actually entertain a conversation with you. Most are bluffing, not just to onlookers but to themselves as well. There's not many worth talking with from what I remember. Really only Admiral Thatch comes to mind."

"I'm still a little unclear how you know her if you're an Ice Hunter. Do you have extensive dealings out of the Dark Lift?" asked Valentina.

"Years ago, yes. But after one too many scuffles over claiming bounties and proper payments, I stopped coming to this side of Europa. It's done wonders for my mental health, and my wallet," laughed Weinwurm before continuing in a somber tone. "Unfortunately, you're going to be thrust right into the wolves' den. I can certainly teach you several cultural norms and a few survival tips, but the only way to survive on the dark side is to remember the very first thing I told you."

Valentina repeated what Weinwurm had said when she first met him, "Always watch your back and trust only yourself, yeah?"

"Yep, you got it. That goes for Thatch as well. She could have drastically changed since the last time I knew her. I only know that she's alive because the Dread Lurkers are still around."

"What are the Dread Lurkers like, exactly? I know they're pirates and that you used to know Admiral Thatch. But am I going to have to actually raid convoys and the like? I'd really like to avoid anything that might actually hurt someone."

Weinwurm considered how best to phrase things before continuing, "I know you're still in shock over what happened in that transport I found you in. But you'll need to deal with those emotions and thoughts before we reach the Dark Lift. That sort of weakness will make you easy to control and manipulate. Europa is the frozen wild west, after all. Most people living here throw out their morals and principals so they can eke out a meager living. So, consider what a person has to do in order to truly thrive in such an environment."

Nothing good came to Valentina's mind. "Now you have me worrying that I won't have anything to bring to the table, and that I'll just end up in a hostage-like scenario to get more credits out of that bastard Wesler. That's what happened the first time I tried to escape from him without properly vetting the individuals aiding my flight."

"That's entirely possible," admitted Weinwurm. "Though from what I gather you're willing to take greater risks if it means staying away from Wesler for even an extra minute. Why do you hate him so much?"

Sighing, Valentina began to explain, "I'll never forget the first time I met him. I was 14. Our two families had worked out an arranged marriage that would not only link the families together but also merge their companies. The combined company would control the lion's share of all shipping and transport between Earth and Luna. There was a lot of pressure on me to like Wesler (or to pretend that I did) for the good of the family. But when he walked into that meeting room and I saw him for the first time, I knew instantly what kind of person he was.

"He was only 16 but carried himself like a king. From his tailored suit to his slicked back hair, this was a man who had thrown away his childhood in order to pretend he could stand shoulder to shoulder with giants. His smile was trained and false, and his eyes were full of the kind of power-tripping rage that your average bully has. Everything, from his voice, his word choice, and body movements, were nothing but business and assertions of his perceived status and authority. The icing on the cake was how his first words to me were 'You will sire me several strong children.' What kind of fourteen-year-old says that? To a twelve-year-old of all people!"

"Not a good one," concluded Weinwurm. "I can only imagine it got worse from there?"

"Indeed, it did. I kept giving him the cold shoulder, only meeting when it was absolutely crucial or I was otherwise forced to do so. Even then, I made it a point to never be alone with him. There was always a trusted bodyguard nearby that I could rely on to keep Wesler's hands off of me. It worked, for the most part. So Wesler did what he thought was the next best thing. He started buying me more and more opulent gifts. Each delivered item carried with it a 'love letter' about how together he would become the head of the richest family in history, and how I should be honored to be the mother of his children."

Weinwurm replied, "Sounds like a real piece of work. From the sounds of it he saw you as a purchasable piece of meat. But one thing isn't tracking for me - how were you able to blow him off for so long? The folks I know like that typically keep escalating until they snap or do something stupid."

"Lying through my teeth, for one," answered Valentina. "I strung him along just enough to keep him wanting more but not desperately so. The major reason, though, was because part of the arranged marriage agreement was that I had to stay a virgin until the marriage was complete. That kept Wesler from actually raping me, but only just. There were definitely moments where I could tell he was just a small push away from trying it anyways."

"That makes more sense to me now," Weinwurm confirmed. "But why run to Europa of all places?"

"Wesler hated the cold. I thought of the farthest and coldest place I could live besides actual deep space. That brought me here. Frankly the fact that he actually came out here just confirms how deranged and obsessed he is about me."

"He definitely sounds like a megalomaniac," agreed Weinwurm. "Which brings me to ask whether you gave my question any further thought? The blind man and the aquarium one."

Valentina mulled it over for a time before replying, "A blind man needs an aquarium to project power. That despite his disability he's able to care for and maintain something that is highly visual in nature. Alternatively, an aquarium is like any other piece of non-audible art to a blind man: something meant to show how well off he is. That he can afford such a testament even if he cannot appreciate it himself. Not unlike how Wesler wants me, I suppose."

"Good answer," Weinwurm started to reply, only for a small light to begin flashing on the control panel of the snowmobile. There were several other vehicles approaching them at high speed from the direction of the Dark Lift.

"Trouble?" Valentina asked nervously.

Weinwurm muttered back, "I don't think so, but be ready all the same."

He pumped the brakes, and within five minutes three other snowmobiles parked a stone's throw away. Thanks to the headlights on Weinwurm's vehicle, Valentina picked out that each had the symbol of a blood-red serpent forming the infinity symbol painted on the side. She tried to remain calm despite the iconography reminding her of a similar logo that Wesler's family used. The lead vehicle asked for face-to-face communication, and moments later the viewscreen of Weinwurm's snowmobile displayed the face of someone that Valentina's gut judged to belong to someone who was accustomed to being a gofer, if only by how serious and confident his eyes were.

"We have been expecting you, Madam Valentina," the man said, completely ignoring Weinwurm. "On behalf of Admiral Chen and the Crimson Serpents, I am here to personally escort you back to the Dark Lift. Grand Admiral Triton has decreed that you are under his personal protection."

"Triton's a big deal," whispered Weinwurm back to Valentina. "He's been running the Dark Lift for decades. If he's offering you protection then you should probably take it. Cautiously, of course. The Crimson Serpents do a lot of business with Ice Hunters. And while I've never known one to use a lie involving Triton before, there's always a first time for everything."

"What assurances do I have that you aren't working for someone else?" Valentina asked the Crimson Serpent representative. "That you really will see me to the Dark Lift unharmed?"

"My word is my bond," replied the man from the Crimson Serpents. "One offered on behalf of Admiral Chen themselves. You need not leave your current vehicle if you would prefer it that way. We will fall in step with you and ensure your path forward is clear."

Despite the risk of trusting this man's word, she reasoned that there would be very little she or Weinwurm could do about it if the Crimson Serpents turned out to be snakes in the grass. "Very well then," Valentina decided. "We'll go as a group to the Dark Lift."

CHAPTER 21

Owen - Oasis Station

Mercenary work turned out to be less difficult than expected for Owen. The Bottom Feeders may have had a fitting name based on the kinds of activities they engaged in, but Owen didn't mind the tasks he was given. The mere fact he had structure to his days once again was enough to make him happy. His jobs involved courier work between parts of Oasis Station, as well as the occasional shakedown. He never knew what he was carrying in the locked duffle bags, only that each run paid well and that he should avoid being caught by station security. This made him believe the parcels were drugs or contraband. Which seemed ironic, given that Oasis Station was a free port on the Dark Side of Europa. Owen had previously assumed places like this had no rules against trade like that.

As for the shakedowns, they got easier as the days went on. At first Owen was met with resistance and exasperated looks from those he was supposed to collect payment from. He learned that all it took was a few knocked over displays and a little roughing up to get most businesses to pay the Bottom Feeder's protection fee.

Owen didn't understand what "protection" the Bottom Feeders were offering at first, given that there weren't multiple competing factions that could actually ruin someone's bar or shop. But one day, when he'd pocketed a payment from a bar owner, he realized that the "protection fee" was basically a predatory tithe to the Bottom Lurkers.

Owen's delay in connecting the dots was due to being sheltered and distracted. His upbringing of living on a mining submarine for nine years limited his exposure to "normal" human interaction. The distractions were due to the snippets of sensation and vision that he received through his mental link with nearby rhadas. None talked to him like the Leviathan had, though. He swore he saw one of the grand beasts every time he passed through a corridor that offered a view outside of the station. Those reports he had overheard from passersby indicated that the rhadas weren't harassing arrivals and departures from Oasis Station like normal. Not even a single swarm had been reported since Owen came aboard.

A full three weeks passed before Owen was called in by his boss, Sven, for an urgent matter. When he arrived at the dregs of the station that the Bottom Feeders called home, a cargo hold turned into a messy living space of third-hand, mismatching furniture and smells of various smokes, he was greeted warmly and with praise.

"If it isn't my top earner," cheered Sven after a jovial clap on Owen's back. "I have good news! It seems your luck is truly astounding! Admiral Kahn will be coming to Oasis Station tomorrow, and he wants to meet with you specifically!"

"That's awesome," returned Owen with a smile. "Though I'm not so sure I'm worth the Admiral's time. I'm just an average bilge rat."

"Do not sell yourself short, my friend! You have a way with people that I'm sure the Admiral wants to capitalize on."

In other words, this is where they'll try and get me back on a submarine so I can help raid people, Owen thought to himself. *And if it's the Admiral asking, I don't think I'll get the chance to say no.*

Then Owen said, "What time should I be here tomorrow?"

"Nice and early!" Sven returned. "But first, you should spend the rest of the night in celebration with me! I've acquired something called a 'rib-eye' and will need help getting through all that meat!"

Whatever the meat was supposed to be, it didn't sit well with Owen's system. Though he suspected that was due to how Sven "cooked" it over his portable grill. Owen spent the night in gastric distress. He was running on fumes by the time of his meeting with Admiral Kahn. Except the Admiral wasn't waiting for him when he dragged himself down to the dregs, only a male courier was.

"Where's the Admiral?" Owen asked cautiously. "I thought I was supposed to meet him here."

"There has been a change of plans," the courier said in a wavering voice. He was skinny, tall, and generally a twig. "The Admiral wants all Bottom Feeders aboard the *Urchin* pronto. That means everyone on Oasis Station."

"Why not tell me that before I drag myself down here?" complained Owen. "Seems like a waste of time for me to have to come all this way to be told I have to trek all the way back up to the docks."

A click of a pneumatic harpoon pistol from behind his head was followed by a gruff voice saying, "Admiral didn't want there to be a record of your body."

In that moment of fear, betrayal, and rage, Owen subconsciously reached out to all the rhadas in the area. There was no way they'd be able to save him from a harpoon from his skull, but maybe they could inflict enough collateral damage in his wake. Time slowed to a stop as Owen waited for the trigger to be pulled.

But it never came. Instead, the courier began speaking into an earpiece much more confidently, "Yeah, we did as you instructed, Admiral. Did it work?" He raised an eyebrow at Owen as he continued, "That many? Should I put you on speaker then? Yes, Admiral."

A tap on the ear brought Admiral Kahn's voice into the space, "So, my dear boy, you thought you had made a clean getaway from the *Sequana*, did you? That we wouldn't find out about your abilities?"

"How... how do you know?" squeaked Owen.

"The Bottom Feeders have eyes everywhere," the Admiral replied. "That bitch Serenity and her Frozen Shadows can't compare to how far we reach. There's always some bilge rat you can rely on to get the information you need. All I had to do was grease a few palms and con a few idiots on the Light Side to get sensor logs and reports from the *Sequana*. Told them I'd be able to claim the bounty on their missing miner. They liked hearing that, and were all too eager to make the exchange without any collateral. Then all that was required to find you was comparing those records to the very obvious transport docked with the station."

Kahn's voice was dripping with excitement and an audible smile as he continued, "You're quite the prize, boy. You're going to make me very, *very* rich. So rich that even the Grand Admiral will be licking my boots."

Before Owen could answer, a sudden whack to the back of his head knocked him out. When he awoke, he found himself in another interrogation room. Only this time there was no Skye to bail him out. He was also handcuffed to the table both by his wrists and his ankles. Waiting for him was the portly Admiral Kahn near the door.

"I'm only going to tell you this once, boy, so listen closely," Kahn said as he leaned over the table towards Owen. His breath was putrid. His jowls quivered like a ribbon in the wind. "You're going to do exactly what I tell you with your xenos puppets. Otherwise, I'm going to start breaking things of yours. I will torture you in ways you can't possibly fathom. Ways that will make you beg for death. But if you do as I say, then maybe I can make sure you get a hot meal now and again."

Owen's worst fears were realized. Once again, his life was out of his control. He felt he already knew the answer, yet he asked anyway, "What are you going to have me do exactly?"

"Simple," growled Kahn. "You're going to help me take apart the Dark Lift piece by piece until the Grand Admiral surrenders. And then? Once I'm the top dog? You'll make sure no one ever double crosses me for fear of a Leviathan eating them. Now, boy, are you going to play nice or do I start ripping off your fingernails?"

"Like you're giving me a choice," Owen spat back. Though not with any amount of gusto. He'd been caught, bound, and caged. And he knew it.

Kahn smiled toothily (albeit with half of the teeth in his mouth missing). "The worst of the worst, boy. And don't forget it. I'll be back when I need you."

The moment the door closed behind the exiting Admiral, Owen struggled against his bonds and roared in frustration. There was only one way out of this situation that he could see, yet he lacked the courage to take it. Nor did he think the Leviathans would actually eat someone they considered to be "blessed by the precursors." That meant he was stuck here. A tool wielded via fear and pain for someone that had his sights set on destruction and domination.

CHAPTER 22
Valentina - Dark Lift

The Crimson Serpents made good on their promise to see Valentina to the Dark Lift unharmed. She would have completely missed the space elevator and its surrounding settlement had it not been pointed out to her. Everything had been made of vantablack material, obscuring the structures not just from sight but from most sensor methods that used the EM spectrum as well. Only the actual station at the top of the space elevator had any running lights, which were barely visible from the surface of Europa. The Crimson Serpents and Weinwurm found their way between buildings with ease and at great speed, like how a commuter knows the streets on their way home. More than once, Valentina expected to crash only for Weinwurm to turn at what she thought was the last possible second. Each time she clenched her eyes shut and braced herself for an impact against an unseen wall.

Such tension was draining, and Valentina was relieved when her ride came to a stop in a vehicle airlock up against one of the tallest spires in the Dark Lift settlement. The Crimson Serpents were forming a corridor for her to follow once she left Weinwurm's care. Before she did, though, Weinwurm had one final bit of advice to give.

"Just because it's the Dark Side of Europa doesn't mean it has to be 'bad' or 'evil,'" he said over his shoulder with a smile. "Don't let others drag you down to their level. Stick to your principles and watch your back. That's how you'll get through this debacle in one piece. Now, go get 'em kid. Send me a message now and again, would ya?"

As the snowmobile's hatch opened, Valentina flashed him a smile and promised, "You've got it. Thank you so much for everything, Weinwurm. I don't know where I'd be without you."

"Probably chained at Wesler's feet," he joked back as she slid out of the vehicle. "But I won't hold it over your head. I only did what someone did for me when I first came here. Remember to show that same kindness one day when you are given the chance."

"You've got it," she replied as the snowmobile resealed. A minute later she'd lost Weinwurm's tail lights amid all the cloaked buildings. She took in a deep breath, held the air in, let it out slowly, then turned to follow the Crimson Serpents to meet this Grand Admiral they had mentioned. One long elevator ride later and she arrived at a shrine that felt severely out of place with what she'd seen of Europa so far. The room was Japanese-inspired, that much was certain. But why a shrine like this was here wasn't clear, nor why there wasn't anyone in the room to meet her.

"If this is a trap, it's been very convincing," Valentina said to her escorts.

"No trap, madam," replied the same man that had opened communication with her. He hadn't provided her a name despite ample opportunity to do so, nor did Valentina feel he would give one if asked. "The Grand Admiral is in the room beyond that wall there. Simply press in at waist level and the door will open."

"Thanks…" she said with a slight sigh. She moved forward and pressed her hand up against the indicated wall. Thankfully, the man's directions helped her only look like a fool for about thirty seconds before she found the hidden panel. It clicked at her touch, followed by the wall sliding away to reveal a dim interior.

"Come inside, Ms. Valentina," urged a sagely voice that she judged belonged to the Grand Admiral. "And ensure the door shuts behind you."

She did as she was instructed. As her eyes adjusted to the gloom, she saw that the space filled from floor to ceiling with holodisplays and readouts. It reminded Valentina of her family's central control hub on Earth with how detailed some of the data was being tracked. As she wandered towards a small spotlight where a robed man sat with his back to her, she remarked:

"I see you appreciate the value of logistics. But where are my manners? Kukleva Valentina Victorovna, as requested. I must thank you for extending your protection to me without even meeting first."

What the Grand Admiral said next was so surprising and frank that it caught her unaware. "I'm dying, Ms. Valentina."

"As in right now or just in general?" she asked as the stunning effect of his words wore off.

"I'm an Admiral, not a General, Ms. Valentina," said Triton.

The Grand Admiral rose and turned to meet her. His single good eye studied her as he clarified, "I have only about three weeks left, Europa-time. Maybe a week more, if that. No one outside this room besides my personal doctor knows. I would prefer it to stay that way, if possible, yet I will not hold you to silence should my proposal not be to your liking."

"I suppose it depends upon your proposal then," Valentina put forth. She almost asked him to come right out and say what was on his mind, but years and years of noble upbringing were coming back to her. The Grand Admiral would get to the point eventually, and couldn't be easily broken from the track he was on.

"Tell me, what do you see in this room?" the Grand Admiral asked.

"The command room of an impressive logistics effort," she answered. "You're tracking everything from crop yields to submarine shipments and orbital transports down to the minutia. Do you manage this all on your own? If so, I must commend you for doing the job of ten men."

"I do get some help now and again," admitted Triton as he brought the sleeves of his loose robe together in front of him. "But yes. Most of what you see is a system I've built since first gaining control of the Dark Lift many many years ago. Without it, the Dark Lift would become a warzone and otherwise be destroyed by all the factions infighting for control. Following me so far?"

Valentina nodded slowly. "You're concerned about leaving a massive power vacuum behind when you pass on. And while I am starting to piece together where this conversation might be going, it wouldn't behoove me to assume."

That got Triton to crack a smile. "Smart and polite. If only more Admirals were like you and Thatch. In any event, the most likely suspicion on your mind is correct. I cannot hand all this over to a single Admiral without risking it all coming apart at the seams. I need a relative outsider that isn't going to be corrupted or otherwise controlled like a puppet. Someone who has some logistics experience and knows what can be outsourced to others. Plus, this will give you real power against that buffoon that's trying to purchase all of Europa to get you back."

"I worry that I am not as talented as you think," she replied carefully. "But I do at least recognize that you've put a great deal of thought into this. When would you need an answer?"

"The sooner the better. End of the day, if possible."

"Then I'll take a walk to ensure I make my decision with clarity, if you'll permit it."

Triton continued to smile warmly back. "I think we both know you've already made the decision. You just need to convince yourself it's the right one. Very well. While in the Dark Lift you are under my protection. All the same, please ensure you have at least one Crimson Serpent with you at all times."

"Of course, Grand Admiral," said Valentina with a deep bow. "I will try to make it a quick walk."

With the guidance of a Crimson Serpent, Valentina found her way to a level of the Grand Admiral's spire that was entirely open in terms of floor plan and furnishings except near the elevators. The empty space looked out onto the Dark Side of Europa, though there wasn't much to see. Which was fine by Valentina. She couldn't afford distractions at this moment.

No matter which angle Valentina approached the Grand Admiral's offer, she could not find fault with it. He was taking a big gamble on her, but not a reckless one. This was the sort of maneuver that a chess master employed when moving their King piece around. The Grand Admiral had ample opportunity and resources to force her to do his bidding. Instead, he approached her like an equal, giving her the chance to decline without fear of reprisal or fall out. The situation was the complete opposite of the backstabbing politics Valentina dealt with back on Earth. Grand Admiral Triton appeared to her as a man that set the example of what a good nobleborn and leader should be. She found it amusing that she had to travel all the way to Europa to find such an individual.

CHAPTER 23
Thatch - Dark Station

Admiral Thatch watched as a late teenager was held up at harpoon point, followed moments later by a sudden and extreme shift in the rhadas behavior around the station he was on. This was followed by the kid being knocked out. The rhadas returned to normal when he fell unconscious and was dragged aboard one of the Bottom Feeders' ships, leading Thatch to a strange yet inevitable conclusion.

"The kid's controlling them somehow," she said to Admiral Serenity in the latter's office within the Dark Lift. "But how is he doing it?"

Serenity switched the monitor to show the teen's dossier, intertwined her fingers before her on her desk, then answered, "That I don't know. Frankly the fact the bloody *Bottom Feeders* beat me to this revelation is embarrassing. The one saving grace to this situation is that Kahn still is an absolute moron when it comes to operational security. Not only do I know where they are keeping this Owen, but I also know that Kahn's been rounding up every single scum and sellsword and buying submarines like they're going out of style. You can probably guess why."

Thatch eyed the report on Owen as she commented, "It's fairly obvious that he's going to make a push for the Dark Lift. If what is on the screen is correct, Kahn's going to use the kid to wrangle up Leviathans and other large rhadas to tie up the defense fleet. Meanwhile all his rats board the Dark Lift and push for control as fast as possible. It's bold, I'll give him that. But it's also stupid. The whole lynchpin of this plan relies on station security and your Crimson Serpents going down easy, and that nothing happens to the kid."

The monitor shifted to show a long-range radar reading stretching out far from the Dark Lift. A large mass of objects were gathering to the southwest. Serenity explained, "Unfortunately, there's enough Leviathans in that bunch to necessitate most of the Crimson Serpents diving in and defending the exterior of the Lift. And even then, the odds aren't in our favor. My best analyst is only giving us a 20% chance of stopping the external assault before the station is damaged beyond repair. That percentage drops to 5% when also considering the matter of halting the interior assault. I'm pulling in nearly every favor I have just to give us a fighting chance. Which leads me to why I called you here to talk in person."

"The Dread Lurkers are ready to assist," Thatch said firmly. "But I have a hunch you have something special planned for us rather than general defense work."

"Sometimes I forget how insightful you are," chuckled back Serenity.

"I did learn from the best, including you."

"Then you should be able to decipher this."

Serenity changed the monitor once more to show a series of force projections moving through simulations in the waters around the Dark Lift. Triangles sized to match the strength of each force collided and clashed in a brilliant display of geometric violence. The largest triangles belonged to the Bottom Feeders, unfortunately. Slowly but surely the sheer numbers were whittling down the station's defenses. That's when Thatch noticed a single small triangle breaking through the front lines and beelining straight for Kahn's sub.

"You want me to lead a strike team to capture the kid," summarized Thatch succinctly. "Again, bold. But the odds aren't good that we'd even get past all those Leviathans and other rhadas, not to mention the Bottom Feeders' second and third lines."

"That's why the Grand Admiral has authorized this plan," smiled Serenity. "Look a little more closely at the strike team's composition."

Thatch did. Then her eyes widened as she realized and replied, "You want us to ride logistics drones like terrestrial Earth cavalry?"

"Exactly. The logistics drones have two benefits," Serenity said as she held up two fingers. "For one: they shouldn't be registered as targets of opportunity. Admiral Kahn might be an idiot but he knows he has to leave as many drones intact as possible to maintain the operation of the Dark Lift should he capture it. The second benefit is that they're easily obscured from the obsolete tech present throughout the Bottom Feeders Fleet."

"That plan is still insane," Thatch pointed out. "All it's going to take is one wrong sonar ping to recognize and/or cripple the drones and their riders. There's also no means of getting back out once Owen's in our control. It's a suicide mission no matter how you look at it."

Serenity turned off the display so there was no distraction from how intensely she eyed Thatch. "Who better to pull off something like this than the favored step-daughter of Triton? Your luck has always been legendary. And lord knows we'll need all the luck we can get for this plan to work. If you're able to get the kid to turn all those rhadas back on the Bottom Feeders then it would be a major boon. But if it comes to it, and you have to kill Owen, there's no telling what the rhadas might do once his control over them vanishes. You and your team would be both the lynchpin and the greatest liability of this plan."

"Time to die in a blaze of glory then," Thatch said, smirking, rising, and extending a hand to Serenity, who did the same. They shook as Thatch continued, "If I don't make it back, I'll trust you to take care of my old man."

"About that… There's actually someone who wants to meet you," Serenity said.

Thatch raised an eyebrow as Serenity tapped a few buttons on her desk to open the office door. On the other side of the threshold was a woman a few years older than Owen. She had a local hairstyle and gear to match, but her posture was of someone still adjusting to Europa's gravity. Thatch also noticed that the woman's eyes were somewhat vacant. The type of thousand-yard, shellshocked stare that lingered after the trauma was long over.

"This is Kukleva Valentina Victorovna," introduced Serenity as she led Thatch over. "Ms. Valentina, this is Admiral Thatch. I've had a meeting room prepared so you two can talk as you requested."

Valentina bowed her head in a manner that instantly confirmed to Thatch that she'd been raised somewhere other than this ice moon. No one paid that much respect to one another on Europa. Even those in the outer colonies on Mars and the Asteroid Belt wouldn't bother with such a notion. Thatch could only conclude that Valentina must be from "old money" back on Earth. Though before Thatch could make a witty comment to that end, Valentina spoke up, "I won't take up much of your time, Admiral Thatch. I just have a few things to say in private before you go."

"Of course," Thatch said with an attempt at the same polite gesture. "Though I doubt Serenity here has any room in this part of the station that isn't bugged or monitored in some way."

A strange look passed between Valentina and Serenity, followed by Serenity replying, "Believe it or not, I can assure you whatever you say in the meeting room will remain there."

Raising an eyebrow at the display of obedience from Serenity, Thatch shrugged and allowed herself to be shepherded alongside Valentina into a smaller room with a single, round table and four rolling chairs. Once the door sealed behind them, Valentina let out a held breath.

"It's nice to finally meet you, Admiral," she said courteously. "I've heard such good things about you from Weinwurm and the Grand Admiral."

Thatch wasted no time in taking a seat, leaning back, putting her boots up on the table, and answering, "So ol' Weinwurm is still dragging his carcass around? I figured he would have kicked the bucket years ago. But we're not here to talk about him, or even me, are we?"

Valentina sighed once more, taking the seat opposite Thatch. "No. I wanted you to be the first person besides the Grand Admiral and Admiral Serenity to know this."

"Awful lot of trust for someone that's likely received Weinwurm's infamous 'everyone is going to stab you in the back' speech. I hardly know you, and vice versa. What is so important and urgent that you have to meet me like this?" asked Thatch.

"The Grand Admiral is dying," Valentina replied plainly, though her somber expression gave away her true feelings on the matter. "And he's putting me in charge of the Dark Lift. Effective immediately once this whole debacle with the Bottom Feeders has been taken care of. I'm sorry, for what it's worth."

Thatch maintained an upbeat tone even as her face tensed up in an attempt to mask her true concern. "I always knew this day would come. Triton couldn't keep on living forever. I also knew he'd never hand over the keys to me or any other Admiral. The job was always going to go to an outsider. The moment he extended his protection to you I had a hunch something was up. He's only ever done that for someone once before, and you're looking at the recipient."

Fidgeting in her chair, Valentina returned, "Yes. It was shocking to hear that he adopted you when you were just a kid. I couldn't believe that such a coincidence had happened. Nor was I prepared for the revelation that Admiral Serenity was the true head of the Sisters of Solace. But that's beside the point."

She leaned in and kept up her cadence, "My family is a logistics powerhouse back on Earth. I'll do my best to keep the lights on and everything functioning as it was prior to the transition. But I'm going to be relying on you and Admiral Serenity for guidance and assistance. At least until I find my feet. Therefore, it was important that I meet with you like this."

"Could have waited until after I returned from certain doom rescuing a kid who apparently can control rhadas," quipped Thatch. "Now I have you to worry about."

Valentina's face flowed into a grimace. "Serenity thought it best I tell you this rather than it coming from her, since it's all connected to me. I'm sure you're aware of my connection to Rolf Wesler and what he's been doing on Europa."

"I know the basics," Thatch admitted.

"Then you should know that if you don't come back, it's not the Bottom Feeders that will actually be in charge of the Dark Lift. Wesler's been pouring funds into their coffers faster than they can spend it. He'll take over the entire moon. And I'll end up as his breeding sow."

Thatch stared in silence at Valentina. Then she swore, "As if politics couldn't get any worse on Europa. You do have a plan for how to deal with him once we win, right?"

"Half of a forming one," professed Valentina honestly. "It relies on you bringing back Owen alive. Wesler may have all the money in the solar system, but he can't buy his way into not getting eaten by a Leviathan. In other words, if we control Owen, we control the moon."

Thatch swung her feet off the table and leaned in as well. "I'll make one thing crystal clear, princess. I don't do slaves or indentured servitude or any bullshit like that. I'm happy to rescue the kid and help him recover, but I'm not going to let you or anyone else just string him along like a puppet."

A smile cracked Valentina's stony expression. "Awful lot of concern for someone you didn't know existed two hours ago. No wonder both the Grand Admiral and Serenity nominated you for this task. I know he'll be in good hands."

"Let's just say he reminds me of someone," Thatch countered as she mirrored the grin. "Any other crap you want to dump on me while we're here?"

"Just one thing: I love the hair."

"Thanks. I see Martha did yours as well."

CHAPTER 24
Owen - E.F.S.V. Urchin

While fear and threats had been enough to control Owen in his defeated state, that still didn't stop the Bottom Feeders from roughing him up every so often. He didn't know why they bothered. He'd long since lost any hope that he would escape, or even see anywhere else besides the inside of this room. The Bottom Feeders were cruel without cause, somehow more mindless and eviler than the rhadas Owen had loathed for nearly a decade.

Owen's only solace was that summoning Leviathans and other large rhadas to the Bottom Feeders fleet gave him someone to talk to. Interacting with them was the only way to break up the monotony of sitting alone in a dark room in pain. The rhadas weren't the best conversationalists but they were better than nothing.

Figuring out their individual voices was challenging for Owen at first. He had to focus on picking out the small idiosyncrasies in word choice and tone in order to pick a specific Leviathan's voice out from the other twenty that were now here. His favorite was one that he'd taken to calling "Sarcasta." Owen didn't think the Leviathans were capable of sarcasm, though everything this one said dripped with it.

[YOU COULD SHUNT THE PAIN TO US. UNLESS YOU PREFER THAT STATE,] Sarcasta said after a session where the Bottom Feeders blackened both of Owen's eyes.

"No, no," Own replied as he grit his teeth through the agony and slumped against one of the walls of his cell. "You're already being controlled like slaves through me. I'm not going to dump my torment on you as well."

[WE HAD NO CHOICE BUT TO COME. THE PROGENITORS SELECTED YOU.]

"About that, what were these 'progenitors' like?"

An image came to his mind across the link of a sea full of light and wonder. Alien settlements far larger and more opulent than anything Europa currently had covered nearly every open thermal vent. Even the smallest settlement dwarfed both Light and Dark Station put together. Glowing tube "highways" connected each community, with hourglass-shaped vehicles rolling through them. The entire ocean floor was illuminated with light and life. The progenitors were blurred shadows a head taller than most humans. Only the xenos (who swam *around* the progenitor vessels without attacking them) and the pyramid-like buildings had noticeable definition in this vision. The abundance of life co-existing

[THEY FILLED THE SEA WITH LIFE,] Sarcasta explained. [AND IN TURN THE LIFE NOURISHED THEM. IT WAS A UTOPIA.]

"They created you? I guess that makes sense given their name. Is that why you xenos are all linked together?"

[THERE IS A CENTRAL INTELLIGENCE AGAINST WHICH ALL THOUGHTS BRUSH. INDIVIDUALITY IS ONLY AFFORDED TO APEX UNITS.]

Owen summarized, "So you have a limited hivemind, with only Leviathans possessing the capability of being unique. This central intelligence, is it the apex of the apex? Where is it located?"

Sarcasta seemed to hesitate as they replied, [UNKNOWN. IT IS BURIED BEYOND THE DEEPEST OF VENTS.]

"I see. What happened to the progenitors then?" Owen inquired. "Why haven't miners found the progenitors' ruins before now?"

[TIME HAPPENED. WE PREVENT THEIR RUINS FROM BEING FOUND. IF A RUIN IS CLOSE TO BEING DISCOVERED THEN WE ACT.]

"Meaning that my encounter with the artifact that gave me this… this power was entirely by chance."

[YOU CATCH ON QUICKLY.]

Sighing, Owen changed topics, "What will you all do once this battle is over? Will you just listen to whatever I tell you to do? Even if someone else is making me give the orders?"

[THE PROGENITORS SELECTED YOU,] repeated Sarcasta without any further clarification.

"But surely since you have free will as a Leviathan you don't want to be told what to attack, what to eat, and so on and so forth?"

[THE PROGENITORS SELECTED YOU,] Sarcasta repeated. Only this time they added, [YOU WOULD NOT HAVE FOUND THEIR LEGACY OTHERWISE. UNTIL YOU ARE CLAIMED BY THE VOID YOU ARE IN CONTROL.]

That was a sobering thought. Owen suspected for quite a while that he could end this entire imminent attack and enslavement of the xenos by paying the ultimate price. But hearing it so plainly like that really made Owen think. He lacked the courage, strength, and willpower to take his own life. Nor had he ever truly cared enough about his fellow man to sacrifice himself for them. That much was known even to the Bottom Feeders. Though perhaps he could use such a fact to his advantage. Sure, he'd likely receive more injuries for his troubles, but that would be ideal. After a certain point Owen's tormentors wouldn't be able to harm him further without risking losing him completely.

Emboldened by these notions, Owen steeled himself for the next time he was visited. Admiral Kahn usually came around after the third "session" to "ask" Owen to summon more rhadas or to issue a command to them via him. And sure enough, the fat bastard appeared a day later. He was sporting a tray with a lavish spread of meats and cheeses, something he deliberately ate in front of Owen to demoralize him further.

"Shame you'll never know how a rib-eye is supposed to be cooked," said Kahn as he chewed the sinew with his mouth open. "Nor how delectable imported muenster cheese can taste."

"I would if you shared," grumbled Owen.

Kahn stopped mid bite to eye Owen. "And give you a reward? For what? You are mine to do with as I wish. I alone control Europa's seas. I have been given providence by the Almighty himself to shape it to my whims."

"You can't even shape your gut," whispered Owen just soft enough that the words were unintelligible to Kahn. Then in a normal voice he went for a longshot, "Then you must be paying your people quite a bit. As far as I know the Bottom Feeders work for the best payouts, even if it means stabbing another in the back."

Kahn finished his bite, set his fork down, then retorted, "That's hardly any of your concern. If you're thinking about offering your guards, or even me, a bribe, then I'll save you the trouble. My coffers are very deep thanks to my business associate."

Though the swelling around his eyes made it difficult to see, Owen still did his best to meet Kahn's eyes. "And what's stopping your 'associate' from just knocking you off when all this is done? Seems to me like you're just as much a puppet as I am."

Kahn's knife embedded in the wall a mere centimeter to the right of Owen's head. "I don't know where you got all this energy to be feisty. One thing *is* clear: You need a reminder who is in control here. Of your current position and lot in life." He pulled out a holoslate from his coat jacket and ordered, "Send out a ping. Maximum yield."

Moments later a ping traveled throughout the ship. At the same time, Owen experienced the agony from all the nearby rhadas as they weathered the sonic attack. The pain was fleeting yet more intense than anything he'd experienced thus far in Kahn's "care." It left him panting and doubled over, sick to his stomach.

"Now then," Kahn continued as he picked up his fork again to resume eating as if he'd swatted a fly. "I've been told that there are several Leviathans that are hanging at the edges of my fleet. Why haven't they joined the main group?"

"Don't know," spat Owen. "Why don't you ask them? Oh. Wait. You need me for that."

This time it was the fork to the left of his head. "Last chance. Why are they hesitating?"

"Probably because of your stench," laughed Owen manically. The mirth of a madman, one with several screws loose. And though it was (sort of) an act, Owen hoped he sold it well enough.

"Two pings this time," Kahn ordered as he watched the effects cause Owen to scream and empty stomach bile onto the floor. Then Kahn picked up the tray and made to leave. "You have two hours to get them to join the fleet. Otherwise, I will personally be at your next session."

Once Kahn was gone, Owen reached out with his mind to try and brush against the aforementioned Leviathans out in the fringes. He didn't get anything coherent back through the link. It was all just noise, like trying to listen to classical music while at a rock concert. So instead, he turned to Sarcasta.

[THEY ARE FRESH FROM THE NEST,] explained Sarcasta once Owen formulated his inquiry. [THEY DO NOT HAVE FULLY-FORMED INTELLIGENCE]

"Babies, children," Owen groaned. "As if this couldn't get any worse. My choice is either to force them into bondage as well, or for me to suffer further torment."

[IT IS YOUR CHOICE TO MAKE.]

Sarcasta's earlier offer of taking on his pain bubbled up in Owen's mind. He might be able to avoid further devastating pings and damage to the rhadas, but there would be no stopping the violence inflicted by the Bottom Feeders on him directly. He'd need help to get through that with his sanity intact.

"Then I'll need you and the other Leviathans to help me bear the pain," Owen grumbled.

[WONDERFUL.]

CHAPTER 25
Thatch, Valentina - Dark Station

Thatch returned to the *Wolffish* immediately after her encounter with Valentina. She had a few loose ends to tie up before she joined the others going on the suicide mission to capture the Owen kid. One was ensuring her affairs were in order in the event she did not come back. The Dread Lurkers were set to slide back into O'Dea's control until he found another protege to take up the head chair. Her wealth would be split evenly between charitable pursuits (mostly orphanages on both the Light and Dark Lifts) and her direct underlings. What personal effects she had were to be put on auction with proceeds going straight to the Dread Lurkers' wallet. Only one big ticket item remained. And for that she'd need Yukawa.

"Yukawa, could you report to my ready room please," she said into her desk terminal.

A quick confirmation and a knock later Yukawa slipped into the room. "You wanted to see me, Admiral?"

"I understand repairs on the *Wolffish* have finished a few days early thanks to your coordination efforts," Thatch began with a soft expression. "Which is great considering the Grand Admiral is going to need all the help he can get in defending the Dark Lift."

Yukawa stepped over the back of the chair, took a seat, leaned in, and reacted, "I had heard rumors that the Bottom Feeders were amassing a gigantic fleet. They're really going to take a run at the station?"

"Indeed. And they're going to have Leviathans and other rhadas helping them," Thatch confirmed. "Or, at least, they will until my mission is complete."

"Whatever the mission is, Ma'am, you have my support," offered Yukawa. "What do you need me to do?"

Thatch paused, took in a deep breath, and glanced once more around her ready room before answering, "I need you to look after the ol' girl for me. There's a high chance I won't be coming back. And even if I'm successful, the only way I'm getting back in one piece is if I steal a sub or have you come to my rescue. So congrats! You're officially promoted to Captain!"

Stunned silence came from Yukawa as he processed the bombs that had dropped on him. He managed to work out, "I'm honored, Admiral. You can be assured I'll take good care of the *Wolffish* while you're gone, and it'll be waiting on your call for help. But are you sure this is for the best? I know you love risks, ma'am, but whatever you're a part of sounds like one hell of a suicide mission. What does it entail?"

"I can't share that unfortunately," sighed Thatch as she stood and moved to shake Yukawa's hand. "However, I am quite sure that I'm putting the right person in charge of this ship. You know her better than I do. The crew looks up to you. Keep on like this and you'll be a proper admiral in no time."

Yukawa also rose and met the offered hand with his own. "This isn't goodbye, Admiral. Make sure of it. Use that luck of yours and do the impossible."

After a firm handshake, Thatch transferred all her command codes to Yukawa and gave him a salute. "The ship is yours, Captain. Congratulations."

Returning the salute, Yukawa completed the change of command by saying, "Thanks, Admiral. For everything."

***

Valentina was partially through calculating which logistics drones could be used for the special operation when an incoming hail popped up on her screen. It had no identifiers attached to it - no name, no frequency, nothing. A true mystery call. Especially considering the console she was using was one of the Grand Admiral's private ones. She figured the hail had to be coming from the Grand Admiral himself or someone he'd trusted enough to reveal the frequency to. However, when she accepted the hail and the console screen displayed who it was, her heart froze for a moment.

"Hello, my queen," Rolf Wesler said. "It's so good to see your face once again."

He was clad in the finest furs and immaculate survival gear that hadn't (and wouldn't) ever seen use. Behind him was the Frozen Skies Resort sitting room. What really caught Valentina's eye, though, was the fact he still had the same slicked hairstyle and devastatingly creepy smile.

"I don't know how you got this frequency, but you can go to hell," Valentina said, finger already in motion towards the button to end the call. "We have nothing to say to each other."

Wesler laughed in a manner that could make milk curdle, "The two most powerful people on this moon have plenty to talk about, my queen. You've captured the Dark Lift, and I the Light Lift. Together we will own and dominate this entire moon AND Earth-Luna travel."

"I haven't captured anything. Nor will I ever work with or marry someone as detestable as you," snarled back Valentina. Wesler had said barely 50 words and her rage was already at a boiling point.

The unnerving smirk on Wesler's face grew as he responded, "That's what makes you truly a queen. You are the only woman to ever give me a challenge like this. I'm utterly captivated by your radiance. I *will* have you, one way or another."

"Not even in your dreams, bastard."

Her finger moved closer to the button but paused as Wesler interjected, "Then what if I made you an offer you couldn't refuse? If you join me at my side then I'll call off the assault. I'll even pull out of the Light Lift and other Europan assets. We'll depart this moon together and leave it to be a frozen hellhole."

Valentina snapped back, "The only pull out that matters is the one your father failed to do with your mother. No deal, Wesler."

"Ah, but you're a reasonable woman! Think of all the lives you could save! All the troubles and damage that our little lover's quarrel is going to cause. Surely you see that you can't win this. You've put up a good fight, my queen, but I will checkmate in two."

"As I recall, I always beat you in those forced chess matches our parents made us play," Valentina replied. "And like those games, you're utterly blind to the truth in your pursuit of me and of victory. So, I will make *you* a deal: Run back home to mommy and daddy with your tail tucked between your legs, and I *might* not humiliate you in front of the entire solar system."

Wesler licked his lips in anticipation, "Such a dirty girl~ Degrading me won't get you--"

The screen nearly shattered with how hard Valentina slammed the disconnect button. She quickly changed the frequency, took a moment to center herself, then returned to her previous work with renewed vigor. The plan had to work. Not just for her sake but for Europa and now all of the solar system.

***

Twenty-five individuals showed up to take part in the suicide mission, including Thatch. Most were members of the Crimson Serpents that Admiral Serenity had hand-picked for this task. But a few oddballs were present in the mix: Two from the Golden Bones and five premiere Ice Hunters. One that Thatch recognized after a moment of processing.

"Weinwurm you old shrew, what are *you* doing here?" called Thatch after slipping into her pressure suit and carrying the helmet under her arm. "Not enough prey topside?"

Weinwurm grunted as he turned mid-suit up, "Apparently not. This is a fool's errand that's going to get us all killed."

"And yet you're here regardless! I always knew you cared about what happens to Europa, despite your claims otherwise," Thatch joked.

"Oh no, that hasn't changed," he replied as he continued to get into his pressure suit. "I still think this moon is the ninth layer of hell. I'd just as soon grab a transport off-world and let the whole thing burn. But I know if I left, I'd regret it for the rest of my life. Right now where I'm needed most is helping you rescue this Owen individual."

Thatch started to reply but paused when she noticed that everyone in the locker room had fallen silent to pay attention to their conversation. She switched tack, announcing to all within earshot, "Let us not forget how important our task is. If we fail, if we don't capture this kid intact, then the life we know will perish. The Bottom Feeders will take over the dark side of Europa, controlling every single movement through their possession of the kid and his rhadas allies. Every struggle we've gone through, every duel, every challenge of fate will have been for nothing.

"But we will *not* fail! Everyone here is the finest that Europa has to offer. Souls brave enough to risk the ultimate price for the hope of a better tomorrow. The blood we spill today will paint the future for this moon! So let us go forth, and take back the life we know! For freedom!"

A loud cheer erupted from the crowd. Even Weinwurm offered a single hoot. Unfortunately, their encouragement was tapered by the Grand Admiral speaking through their helmets, announcing, "Strike team, this is Grand Admiral Triton. Contact in thirty minutes. Prep for departure."

"You heard the man! Let's do this!" roared Thatch as she firmly fastened her helmet in place.

CHAPTER 26

Thatch, Owen - Dark Lift

The submerged underside of the Dark Lift lit up like a Christmas tree as innumerable defenses came online. Torpedoes, sonic weapons, and articulating arms prepared to fend off anything that broke past the front lines. Meanwhile countless strike craft launched from both station and submarine alike to fill the sea with more lights. Mixed among them were Thatch and her team, riding logistics drones like cowboys in their pressure suits. All gathered forces formed several battle lines and waited for first contact.

"They're sending in the Leviathans first," Yukawa informed Thatch from the *Wolffish* bridge via one-way transmission. "Along with a volley of torpedoes. Godspeed, Admiral."

Sure enough, the cacophonous bellows of multiple Leviathans filled the water as the creatures' bioluminescent sides flared crimson on their approach. Behind and around the sea serpents were a multitude of torpedoes. Beast and projectile together formed a deadly swarm that gave Thatch a moment's pause.

"Steady people," she said over comms to her team. "We go after the counterswarm measures have struck."

Moments later the allied fleet unleashed their own flock of torpedoes. Both bevies raced towards one another with blistering speed. Then the first projectile exploded. Concussive blasts echoed throughout the ocean as bright detonations eliminated swaths of torpedoes and dealt blows to the Leviathans. Several of the gargantuan creatures and underwater rockets made it through, slamming into the allied fleet like a crashing wave.

Metal screeched. Sonic weapons blew out compression waves. Vibrochainsaws revved, ripped, and tore. Leviathans snarled. Torpedoes filled the ocean. Flashes of light cast shadows and impressions of the dead in a melee unlike any other that Thatch had been a part of. One she barely heard herself over as she commanded her team forward, "Go! Now! Don't get caught! Our goal is Admiral Kahn's sub! Stop for nothing else!"

Thatch kicked her drone into high gear as she and her team streaked towards the enemy fleet. They were met first by a horde of small craft and medium-sized xenos, either they didn't notice the drones or were too focused on their mission of boarding the station to scan the drones. The plan was proceeding smoothly until Thatch's team reached the second line of ships.

A loud ping joined the din coming from behind them at the Dark Lift, followed by Kahn's forces beginning to deploy anti-diver weaponry. Five members of Thatch's team were gibbed instantly. Ten more were crippled and sent spiraling either down towards the seabed or up into the ice. Of the fifteen that remained, only seven plus Thatch ever made it far enough to see the *Urchin*. By the time Thatch's drone made contact with the *Urchin*'s hull, only three of her team remained.

The repurposed logistics drones lanced through the metal plating to open up entry points for the strike team. Every second they worked was another moment of borrowed time. Would they finish and allow the strike team to slip inside? Or would the sonic weapons recharge in time to swat them off like flies? Such thoughts nagged at Thatch as she urged her drone to go faster, though words were lost on the automated unit.

Time seemed to stretch on forever. The drones were cutting too slowly. A sonic blast was imminent if Thatch's mental stopwatch was right. Then a bulkhead popped, spilling out air and filling the space with water, then another. The drones clustered together and formed a barrier as Thatch and her team moved inside the *Urchin* just as a decimating ping tore through the nearby waters.

Looking around, Thatch saw that it was Weinwurm, the two Golden Bones, and herself against an entire submarine. *Unfair odds*, Thatch thought. *They'll need twice that to challenge me.*

***

Despite the defender's best efforts, a multitude of strike craft managed to hard dock with the Dark Lift. They crowded and jostled for any room to clamp down and cut through the hull like piranhas. Station security outfitted with flechette launchers, lancejets, and gold-colored, armored bodygloves bearing an azure icosahedron on the chest met the comparatively unequipped, untrained, and unwashed forces that poured out from these assault boats. The Bottom Feeders were hoping to overwhelm station security with sheer numbers. For every two of the Bottom Feeders that died, another five took their place. Whereas the forces aboard the station felt every loss of personnel and barricade to the hailstorm of fire from the mob. The Bottom Feeders used a multitude of underhanded tricks and cheats to gain ground, ranging from children soldiers, hostages used as meat shields, and use of high-caliber weaponry that breached the hull and led to explosive decompression. Further brutal was that outright death was a luxury only a few were permitted. The injured dropped in place with their bodies filled with metal flechettes, only to be trampled or otherwise crushed as the Bottom Feeders pushed forward. Limbs were blown off or turned into swiss cheese. Blood flowed so freely that the decks were turning into comical slip n' slides.

Station security knew this was a fight they could not win. They had the more deadly and efficient weapons but they were slowly pushed back. The first line of defense, the Dark Lift's main promenade to which all docks connected, fell in less than an hour. The space was too big and the Bottom Feeders too numerous for station security to hold onto for long. Many of the shops, bars, and other businesses were turned into chaotic, ruined messes as station security pulled back. They were forced to retreat behind a series of collapsing bulkheads between the inner and outer rings that were designed to prevent hull breaches from decompressing the station. This bought the defenders some time, but at the cost of allowing the attackers to fan out and probe towards the Dark Lift's central lifts and control rooms. Soon station security was beset on nearly every side by attacks, rather than one unified push from a single direction. They were forced to begin severing the cables and lines to the lifts, severing both means of access and of escape.

Heroic and desperate last stands became commonplace. By the time the Bottom Feeders reached the main lifts, only 35% of the defenders remained. Things were looking grim as the Grand Admiral watched on from his command center. Yet everything was going according to plan.

A second line of bulkheads came crashing down before the main lifts, followed by the transmission of a signal ping. Moments later reserved squadrons of allied strike craft cut through and excised the Bottom Feeder's assault boats from the station's hull. The result was water slamming and tearing through the corridors of the station that hadn't been sealed up. In other words, the areas in which the Bottom Feeders were concentrated. A lucky few Bottom Feeders managed to dive into side rooms and seal themselves in, but over half of the attackers were consumed and drowned in the ensuing torrent.

The next wave of the Bottom Feeders' assault arrived before the station defenders could celebrate for long. The controlled-rhadas used the new water passageways to get inside the station and begin eviscerating the interior with beaks, claws, and other destructive implements. Station security relied on sonic weapons and controlled explosions to keep the worst of the rhadas at bay. But as much as they were holding, every defender knew that it wouldn't last forever. They just prayed that they lasted long enough to see the fruits of Thatch's secret mission, whatever it was.

***

The first group aboard the *Urchin* that Thatch and her team encountered went down in a hailstorm of flechette rounds. As did the second. The element of surprise and the general unpreparedness of Admiral Kahn's crew meant that Thatch's team was sweeping through the decks like a tornado in a trailer park. The tight corridors forced their initial opposition into barrages of shrapnel and sparks. Despite their progress, Thatch's team knew that soon the *Urchin*'s crew would muster a proper defense and stop them dead. Literally.

Crucial minutes of Thatch's operational window were being lost. One of the Golden Bones went down from a lucky headshot that pierced out the back of his helmet. His comrade spectacularly avenged him, grabbing up the fallen flechette rifle and dual wielding them as Thatch and Weinwurm broke through another security door with a code breaking unit. This brought the team to a T-shaped intersection with a corridor ahead and to the right of them.

"The kid should be in one of these rooms," Thatch shouted as she motioned at the passageway to the right.

Weinwurm nodded, then used a mirror to peek around the corner. Sure enough, a whole squad of heavily-armed Bottom Feeders was waiting outside one of the brig rooms at the end of the hallway. He reported this to Thatch, adding, "Think it's safe enough for a grenade? I've got 3 flash bangs and 5 frags in my pack."

"Whatever you do, do it fast!" called the surviving Golden Bones member from behind them. "I'm running out of ammo and they just keep coming!"

It was risky as all hell. An explosion in confined spaces like this could inadvertently harm the kid they had come all this way to get. Even a flash bang could do serious damage to the unprotected. But Thatch didn't have the time or resources to break through the miniature barricade that lay between her team and their prize.

Thatch made a split-second decision. "Do it," she said to Weinwurm. "Start with flash bangs if you've got 'em."

Weinwurm produced two white cylinders, pulled the pins, then threw one underhand and rolled the other on the floor towards the waiting Bottom Feeders. An extremely bright flash of light and thunderous sound followed, then Thatch and Weinwurm turned the corner and unleashed hell on their stunned foes.

"Take these and help out Golden Boy," ordered Thatch as she scooped up the dead Bottom Feeder weapons and handed them to Weinwurm. She turned to begin breaking into the cells, but Weinwurm hadn't moved. "There something wrong, Weinwurm?"

"We don't have time to get the kid to a fresh pressure suit," Weinwurm said, already reaching up to unseal his helmet. "Nor do we have time to go back to our entry point or to an airlock. That means you're going to need this."

Thatch paused her work, looking through her visor with a forlorn expression. She knew he was right. Maybe if more of their team had made it aboard, they could have secured an exit route. Now all that remained for an exit strategy were the fragmentation grenades in Weinwurm's pack.

"I'm sorry," she offered simply as Weinwurm fully divested himself from the pressure suit. "Even my legendary luck couldn't hold out forever."

"Not your fault, girl," he replied as he handed her the suit. Then he picked up the weapons and his pack, moving towards where their last team member was holding. "Just make sure you include my heroic sacrifice when you tell this story. Fluff it up a bit. Give me some injuries. Make it something people talk about for decades."

Thatch nodded, "Give 'em hell, old man."

***

Owen was only aware of the explosions outside of his cell thanks to the inordinate amount of pain flowing through the mental link he had with the rhadas. The agony coming through was more crippling and blinding than the flash bangs that had gone off. Every single centimeter of skin, every muscle and bone, every neuron in his body were firing in agony. That Owen was aware of the walls of his cell was a small wonder.

A new beacon of light entered Owen's torment in the form of an angel. Her entire body was made of light as impossibly-large, feathered wings fanned out behind her. She beelined for Owen, slicing his restraints before roughly picking him up and wrangling him into a pressure suit.

"Just… kill me…" he mumbled, eyes fluttering. "Can't hold on…"

"Not an option, kid," said the angel's voice. "You die here and everything goes to shit. Stay with me. We're almost out."

"Out? How?"

The angel didn't give him a verbal answer. Instead, she clicked his helmet into place, ensured it had pressurized properly, then lay over him on the floor. Moments later a shockwave of light, sound, and fire tore through the corridor. It blew not just the door of his cell open but also a hole in the side of the *Urchin*. Water came roaring in and filled the space within seconds. Owen didn't have the strength to move, but his rescuer did. Soon the two of them were drifting away from the submarine as it continued towards the Dark Lift.

"You still with me, boy?" said the angel as she pressed her helmet up against his. He managed to nod, to which she carried on, "We need you to call off the rhadas, or at least get them to start attacking the Bottom Feeders. Then we'll just have to hope someone can rescue us before Kahn discovers you survived and pings us to death."

"I can… do that," Owen panted. All it took was a few seconds of thought for the writhing serpents in the distance to switch targets. "There. I don't think I can get a Leviathan to pick us up. They're all too injured to break through Kahn's defensive line."

"Could you get them all to follow a couple of ships in particular?" the angel asked. "One of them is going to be very easy to spot…"

***

Admiral Kahn's plan was falling apart around him. The xenos he'd been relying on were turning on him and his Bottom Feeders thanks to that witch Thatch killing Owen. He still had the advantage in numbers, though most of the remaining boats he had were simple torpedo boats and assault craft. Surely, he could think of a way out of this mess. Or if not, maybe he could pull back and try again another day?

To make matters worse, an incoming communication interrupted his thoughts. When he brought it up on his command chair, the voice of Rolf Wesler filled the bridge.

"How goes the operation, Admiral?"

"It's gone to shit," swore Kahn as he slammed his fists onto the armrests of his chair. "I told you we should have waited longer and gotten more reinforcements! Now my xenos conduit is gone and the Dark Lift is holding!"

"Perhaps if you used the Owen child more effectively you wouldn't be in such a mess," mused Wesler, as if he were observing a spec of dirt on his fingernail. "But it is of no great consequence. Finding one alien device to create a xenos conduit means that there may be others out there to find. We can always start anew."

"Maybe *you* can, but I staked everything on this!"

"One wonders how you became an Admiral with such poor tactics."

"Why you--!"

The communication cut off right as one of Kahn's crew shouted, "Sir! Every single Leviathan is coming right for us! And at their head is the *Wolffish!*"

Another yell came, "Torpedoes in the water sir! We don't have time to evade with all the water we've taken on!"

Kahn stood up, commanding, "Well then launch counter torpedoes! Turn us away from the projectiles to present a smaller silhouette!"

"Trying, Sir! But--!"

A flechette round silenced the man before he could finish the protest. But the round hadn't come from Kahn's pistol. Instead, it came from someone Kahn had never met before stumbling onto his bridge. He was old, weathered, with so many needles sticking out of him and so much blood dripping from his wounds that he shouldn't have been able to stand, let alone breathe.

"Shame Thatch didn't get to see this bit," grunted Weinwurm as he took out several more of Kahn's bridge crew. Kahn himself put the old man down with a careful shot, but the damage was done. There was not enough time and people left to avoid any of the incoming barrage.

The torpedoes connected. Nearly every alarm began blaring on the bridge as sparks spewed from consoles and main power was lost. Moments later, three Leviathans coiled around the fractured tin can that was the *Urchin* and crushed it into scrap.

CHAPTER 27
Owen, Thatch, Valentina - Dark Station

The next thing Owen knew was that he was lying on something soft. A weighted blanket provided pleasant pressure across his form, while a machine off to his right beeped in tune with his heartbeat. He guessed he was in a medbay, though lacked the strength to open his eyes and confirm it. The best he could manage was breathing and listening intently to his surroundings. This allowed him to pick up a conversation happening nearby.

"It's a miracle he's in one piece," said a man with a voice like gravel. "He's looking at months of recovery time just to heal his physical wounds. I can't speak to his mental ones other than to say his neurochemistry is all over the place. But based on what you've told me so far, we'd be lucky if he didn't go catatonic."

"Then we have to hope he retains his sanity," replied a woman in a refined, yet firm, manner. "The fact the Leviathans haven't attacked us further is a good sign that he will pull through."

Then the voice of the angel joined in, "He's a tough kid. The fact he was still conscious when I found him speaks to his strength. He'll pull through."

"Were we all optimists like you, Thatch" sighed the first woman. "I don't know how you remain so upbeat. Sure, we won the day and the Dark Lift is safe. But at what cost?"

"Worry about that later," Thatch replied. "Focus on the now. I know you're hurting over Weinwurm, but he gave us this opportunity. We shouldn't squander it."

The man (who Owen was guessing was his doctor) interrupted, "Ladies, I believe our patient is awake."

He may not have been able to open his eyes, but Owen still managed to croak, "Barely. But yes. I need to stop waking up in sickbays."

The sounds of shuffling were followed by the three voices coming from around his bed. "Do not pressure him too much," cautioned the doctor. "Marvelous as this is, you should avoid putting more stress on him."

"He'll be fine," chuckled Thatch. "Ain't that right, kid?"

Owen coughed back, "Debatable. Where... am I?"

The unknown woman answered, "You're aboard the Dark Lift, specifically in the part above the ice. My name is Administrator Valentina. I have my best doctors looking after you."

"And what about... the rhadas?" inquired Owen. "I can't feel them as much anymore."

"That's because you're heavily medicated at the moment," the doctor informed Owen. "The theta waves produced by your brain are being limited."

Thatch chipped in, "We know you're still connected because a bunch of the surface rhadas have been crowded around the base of this tower for several days. And because the Leviathans in the ocean below have generally been helping mop up the last Bottom Feeder holdouts."

"Then... could you shut off the connection completely?" Owen asked as the idea crossed his mind.

"Potentially with study, but not likely," admitted his doctor. "You've formed far too many neural connections at this point. To suppress or remove them would be like removing your ability to see or the ability to walk."

Sighing, Owen grumbled, "Maybe that's what Skye meant with the blind man and the aquarium. I either cripple myself to watch on passively or I'm stuck with them, then. Great. I guess you're better hosts than that fat bastard."

There was a moment of pause before Valentina said, "Yes, well, that's something we do need to address at some point. You don't have to make a decision now, but you do deserve to know where we stand."

"Let's hear it then," Owen urged. "But from the angel who saved me."

Valentina snickered as Thatch replied, "Going to stop you there, kid. I'm no angel. But I'll give it to you straight: You're in very high demand right now. The administrator here wants to offer you a safe harbor and place to recover in the hopes you'd be willing to work with her in interfacing with the rhadas. But as I've made abundantly clear to her several times, you're under no obligation to stay here once you're back to fighting shape. It'd make things rough in dealing with our new problem, but we could figure something out. We always do."

Owen took his time processing those words, turning them over in his foggy mind as he tried to search for any double meanings or omitted details. Either there were none or he lacked the current faculties to discern them. Therefore, he countered, "If I'm going to stay here long term, I'm going to want a few things."

"Of course," assured Valentina. "What is it you want?"

"For starters, I want a rib-eye. A properly cooked one. And a big mug of the best beer you have."

[THAT SEEMS UNNECESSARY], Sarcasta chimed in, somehow getting through to Owen's heavily medicated mind.

"Shut up, Sarcasta."

His doctor asked, "Pardon?"

"Just telling a Leviathan to mind its own business."

***

Valentina and Thatch left Owen's bedside together and made for Valentina's office. She'd kept most of the Grand Admiral's decorations up after he turned the keys over to her, only adding a picture of Weinwurm on the wall behind her desk in memoriam. Once both women were seated, Thatch was the first to speak:

"Have you given more thought to my proposal? I don't need an answer right away, but I do need it soon."

"Repairs on the station are going to take months to complete," replied Valentina. "I can hardly spare my engineers to help you design a new kind of submarine. *However*, I do recognize that you've performed a great service. Not just for the Grand Admiral, myself, or even the people who live on the Dark Lift. You've helped prevent Wesler from winning. And that, in my book, is worth almost any price."

"So, my request…?"

"Granted. On two conditions: You name the ship class *Weinwurm*, and you put every bell and whistle you can think of on it. If we're going to be crafting a dreadnought, I want it to be something that makes even a Leviathan afraid."

Thatch laughed and winked at Valentina, "Not that we have to worry about that much, given the kid just wants food, beer, and a VR suite for himself. And a happy kid means happy rhadas."

"About that," exhaled Valentina. "The records I've seen of his past life indicate he's a workaholic. Eventually I'm going to have to give him a proper job other than being a conduit to the xenos. Not that that should be hard to find on the Dark Lift, yet I worry he'll try and follow you around like a lovesick puppy."

"Bah, he'd better not," dismissed Thatch. "I'll shut him down hard if he tries."

Valentina smirked then added, "Still, I have a feeling that the more we learn about the xenos through him, the more we'll have to risk him leaving the Dark Lift. I just hope we're able to finish recreating the fleet before Wesler does on his end. That includes beefing up orbital encampments in case he tries to come in that way."

"You handle the sky, Serenity can handle the ground, and I'll handle the sea," Thatch proposed. "The kid can bounce between us as needed. Deal?"

"Deal."

***

The Grand Admiral's funeral was one week later. Thatch and Valentina had spent what time they could spare at Triton's side until he finally passed on. The two women plus every Admiral and connection still worth their salt attended the grand affair in one of the large hangars normally reserved for ship repair. Banners with the double Leviathan hung next to images of Triton as his body laid in a torpedo casing before a small stage. Thatch had the microphone first.

"Today we honor the passing of a man that took me in when I was most vulnerable," she began. "Someone who saw a crying child and decided to do something about it instead of ignoring her and continuing on his way. That's the kind of man Triton was. Someone who saw problems and worked to fix them, rather than create more. He made it very clear in his dying days that we shouldn't be mourning his passing. Instead, we should celebrate what he gave us. This station. Our way of life. Freedom that no one else in the solar system can match. We may be on the 'dark side' of the moon, but we need not give into such dark impulses like the Bottom Feeders did. Triton would want us to band together as one large family. Though maybe not for Thanksgiving. I don't want to hear all your crazy uncle stories."

That got a laugh from a majority of those present. Thatch then saluted Triton's body and tacked on, "Give them hell in the afterlife, Dad."

A bosun sounded his whistle as the torpedo casing sealed and loaded into a tube. Moments later it fired out into the murky depths and disappeared from view. After giving the crowd a minute or so to lament, Thatch turned to look at Valentina and said, "Now then, Triton has given the crown to our newest Administrator here. Some of you don't like that, to which I say: Tough. She'll do a fine job if you assholes don't try and assassinate her every day that ends in 'y' like you did with Triton. But I'm just a salty sea dog. Let's hear it from the Administrator herself!"

Thatch and Valentina switched places, the Administrator muttering sarcastically, "Thanks for riling them up." Once at the microphone, Valentina cleared her throat and spoke, "The truth is that I'm not Triton. Nor will I ever be able to fully replace him or even fill out his shoes. But what I can do is commit to keeping the Dark Lift an open port of call for anyone that agrees to the rules he put out. Which is why I have something special to share with each and every admiral present."

The crowd leaned in expectantly, whispering excitedly. Valentina carried on to say, "Triton used your tithes to further scientific developments and research. He also invested a fair amount into the solar markets. So, in short, here's the good news: Every Admiral will receive a technological overhaul for their vessels so that everyone is on a level playing field. And I mean *every* vessel in your fleet. Free of charge. Well, you'll still have to pay docking fees, and there will be an *orderly queue*, but other than that, free. Maybe that'll help convince you I'm worth keeping around?"

An admiral in the front row stood up and began to cheer. The rest of the crowd quickly followed suit as Valentina bowed and stepped away from the podium to give way to Serenity. Something grand had started, despite the danger still looming over Europa...

CHAPTER 28
Wesler - Light Station

Rolf Wesler looked down upon the icy, scarred surface of Europa from his new home on Light Station. He'd bought out the Frozen Skies Resort and turned it into a palace fit for the king he was. Likewise, he had taken over a majority of the Light Lift's logistical companies and contracts using the weight of his name and of his wallet. Nothing moved up or down to Europa on the light side without him knowing about it. His intelligence network was growing by the day, and by all accounts he would soon have a monopoly on light side mining ventures both terrestrial and aquatic.

So why, then, did he feel like he was missing something very important?

The answer was simple. He lacked the one thing that apparently money *couldn't* buy: the affection of his queen. Not only she made a mockery of him, but reports of what had transpired on Europa had reached Earth. He was a laughing stock, even among his family. Though he cared little. He was the heir to the Wesler fortune regardless, and with time proper respect could be reestablished. What mattered to him in this moment was how to reach his beloved Valentina.

"Pardon me, Sir," said a butler as they announced themselves. "You wished to know when the report about the Midnight Hearts incident was available."

"Bring it here," Wesler replied, holding out a hand to his side without bothering to turn away from the window. A holoslate was placed into his hands and the hired help departed.

He casually glanced over the report currently on screen. Several Ice Hunters had managed to track down the xenos that had ransacked the Midnight Heart's main mining site, the same incident that almost saw him capturing his queen had his agent not failed at the last moment. Regardless, the Ice Hunters had extracted an artifact from amidst the xenos and were currently on their way back to the Light Lift. Wesler quickly thumbed up until an image of the artifact was on screen.

"Well, aren't you a beautiful thing," he mused as he also pulled up an image of the relic that Owen had found months ago. The two were nearly a perfect match. The only difference was the alien symbol work found on the fronts. "You are going to let me finally capture my queen..."

APPENDIX A - Important Terms, Slang, and Definitions

A day on Europa is 84 hours long. This means a week on Europa is equivalent to 24.5 days on Earth. **Unless otherwise specified, all time measurements are Europa-local.**

The icy surface of Europa as a whole is known as the **Carnus Expanse**.

Sea of Sarpedon is the name for the ocean that lies beneath the ice crust of Europa. The Dark Side of the sea is sometimes referred to as the **Minos Mire**, while the Light Side can be called the **Alagonian Depths**.

Rhadas (short for Rhadamanthys) is what Europan locals call the alien lifeforms native to the moon. Off-worlders tend to refer to the aliens as **xenos**.

Made in the USA
Middletown, DE
18 November 2022

15305686R00115